Please Stay on the Trail:
A Collection of Colorado Fiction

Black Ocean
Boston - New York - Chicago

Compiled and edited by Matt Hudson
Design by Heather Sutphin

To reprint, reproduce, or transmit electronically, or by recording all or part of *Please Stay on the Trail*, beyond brief excerpts for reviews or educational purposes, please send a written request to the publisher at:

BLACK OCEAN
P.O. Box 990962
Boston, MA 02199
www.blackocean.org

Library of Congress Cataloging-in-Publication Data

Please stay on the trail : a collection of Colorado fiction / compiled and edited by Matt Hudson.
p. cm.
Includes bibliographical references.
1. Short stories, American--Colorado. 2. American fiction--21st century. I. Hudson, Matt, 1978-

PS571.C6P54 2006
813'.01089788--dc22
2006000924

Printed and bound in the United States of America.
FIRST EDITION

"Train Going Away" by Chris Ransick. First published in his collection *A Return to Emptiness* (Ghost Road Press, 2005), and reprinted by permission of the author.

"In the Slatted Light" by A. Rooney. First published in *The Colorado Motet* (Ghost Road Press, 2005), and reprinted by permission of the author.

To A

Contents

Forward

As the cover might suggest, I do a lot of hiking. From the hot, Sahara-like sand-scape of Great Sand Dunes National Park to the cloud-kissed heights of the Never Summer Wilderness, I'm consistently awed by the range of experiences Colorado offers. I've come to expect that, whatever trail I head out on, however familiar the terrain may seem, every trail offers a new experience. It might be a mother moose calmly staring into the pines, or maybe even a hidden high-mountain lake atop a long, dusty trail, but usually by the end of the trip I've discovered something I hadn't expected. Sometimes on a hike you just want to get to the end, but on a good hike, when the trail is taking you someplace you've never been, and when you find a certain rhythm in your movements that puts your mind at ease, when you get to the end, you don't want to leave. In that way, a satisfying hike bears a lot of similarities to a well-written story. both involve effort and exploration and both offer a certain degree of discovery and emotional payoff.

As a writer, when I first arrived in Colorado I went into a bookstore hoping to find a collection like this, a sampler of local authors. At the time I could only name a handful of Colorado-based authors—Clive Cussler, Hunter S. Thompson, Pam Houston, and Rikki Ducornet—but I knew there was a much deeper writing community here and it didn't take a whole lot of digging to find it. It seems like every mountain town I have traveled through has its own writers group: Aspen, Telluride, and Steamboat are just a few. More than twenty Colorado universities and colleges teach fiction writing, several of which publish their own highly regarded literary journals. Programs like the Lighthouse Writers Workshop also offer an array of fiction writing classes. Numerous publishers are scattered throughout the state. Denver's Ghost Road Press has published many Colorado authors, including several of whom are included here.

I never found a collection like this, and when I didn't, I did some research and de-cided to create one. To begin, I sent requests for submissions to every Colorado-based author and university I could find. When someone recommended authors, I tracked them down and encouraged them to submit something too. I posted signs in coffee shops, bookstores, and libraries. Soon, submissions poured in from around the state.

In compiling this collection, I've attempted to put together a different sort of guide to Colorado's terrain. Initially I set out to create *the* Colorado collection, a definitive anthology full of Colorado's finest authors. What I discovered is that Colorado's creative talents couldn't possibly be contained in one book. This is *a* Colorado collection. Of these ten stories, some stood out because of their palpable physical description, others had humor or emotional intensity. Overall, these short stories and novel chapters represent only a small sample of Colorado's literature. I encourage you to stay on the trail; discover Colorado's rich writing talent.

Matt Hudson
January 7, 2006

Thrashing

By Teague Bohlen

It was fall, and fall meant thrashing. The old traveling thrasher crews had appeared again like spring corn, as more and more farmers found themselves with less and less money to purchase their own equipment, or to repair what they already had. So the first thrashers, the mobile tank-like monsters of old technology, were brought out again, fired up for the first time in decades, repaired, greased, and put on the road and up for hire. They were huge things, all gears and belts and teeth the likes of which gave any sane man cause for extreme care, but invariably, they were manned by either boys or desperate men, both of whom were willing to work long hours for short pay. Reese Moss was the former, Tom Horseman the latter. On the thrasher together, they became friends that autumn of 1932, bound by common labor, and, near the end of the fall, by common tragedy.

Reese was sixteen when he was hired on the crew, a boy whose father still worked the Moss family fields, and who had little to pass onto his son but a willingness to work. And work Reese did, though often more out of a sense of love rather than duty or ethic. Reese loved the smell of the fields, especially in the autumn, when everything is finishing its slow but certain arc toward use. Kernel to leaf to stalk to husk to plate—that was the way of things. Everything he did, in his eyes, was important to someone, and he relished being part of that process. He liked the idea that the beans he walked became someone's noon soup, or the corn he detassled became someone's supper, roasted and slathered in butter and honey, like his mother used to make. He knew enough about crops to know that these visions were nothing but—the beans were processed into oil, and the corn was mostly feed corn, fit for only livestock, but the vision was what counted. He was doing something, he convinced himself, and the thrasher was the final part of it. The golden part, really, with the chaff floating in the air and the yellow blur of field after field after field. It smelled like life, Reese thought. He told this once to Tom, who had laughed at him. It wasn't life, Tom had said. Just the opposite. Everything around you is dying, he had said, clearing his throat and spitting into the stalks.

Reese paid him no mind. Tom was like that, Reese had learned. He and Tom had found themselves running in the same circles those past few months, looking for work, and they had often found it together. They had walked beans together out near Taylorville, worked a hay baler near Bethany, and had found themselves, most recently, feeding the thrasher with nothing but pitchforks with good tines and backs with strong heave. So they came to know each other as men who labor together often do—each knew the rhythm of the other's movement, and could plan his around it. After a short time, they found themselves spending what small money they earned together as well.

They had been working the thrasher all over Illinois, finding jobs at one farm and then the next, and their work had led them right back home to Moweaqua. They had both been born there, and both knew the town well—the streets, the stores, the ways of people and the people themselves. When they returned it seemed to them as though they might receive some homecoming, a parade possibly, for Moweaqua's favorite sons, home from the outlying fields, men who had dared to brave the plains of the state, to survive outside the comfort of home. People would give them free coffee with sugar cubes, and possibly even hire them on at their farms. It would be just like the men coming home from war.

Or at least, this was Tom's idea. Reese let him talk, as usual, but silently thought that it would be enough just to sit in the shade of the elm near his house again, or go down to Stroh's Pool Room on Main just to hear the old ivory balls clicking together sharply over the low murmur of the men who gathered there. Stroh's was the most indecent place in town—had been even before Prohibition—and Moweaqua men loved it for that. It was the only place for miles that never took to the Volstead Act, and boasted a supply of whiskey readily available upstairs where they set up the duck pins. It was almost always full. It was also where fathers brought their boys on their twelfth birthdays, to buy them licorice whips and horehound candy from Ben Hudson's Drug and Ice Cream across the street, and to let them sit in the line of chairs against the north wall, the ones raised up on a short step to better see the green felt of the tables, and watch how the balls rolled over it like water on greased metal. The fathers would show off their boys, nodding to them and winking while in conversation with the other men, and, right before they would go back home, would show the boy how to hold a cue. It was what Reese's father had done for him almost four years before, and Reese remembered every second of it, the smell of tobacco, the smooth wood of the chair, the taste of the root beer his father had bought him and then made him promise not to tell his mother about. Reese saw himself doing the same for his boy, sometime, whenever he had a boy, that is, but he thought of it whenever he went into Stroh's Pool Room, whenever he racked the small, perfectly round balls, whenever he tasted licorice. This was what Reese looked forward to in going back home. This, and little more.

Tom had no family to speak of anymore—he was the only son of immigrant parents, and his mother had died in childbirth. His father had supported them, for a time, working odd jobs around town, finally landing permanent work in the Moweaqua coal mine, a big operation for a town of any size, let alone a small place like Moweaqua. It was a deep mine with a coal house and tipple atop the shaft, and it employed nearly one hundred and fifty men on average. Tom's father worked there until 1926, when he was killed, crushed under falling slate. Tom was sixteen, and lived on his own, in a shanty-house his father had bought and built-up, following in his father's footsteps, working odd jobs. He swore that he would never set foot in the mine, that it was a bad place. Once, while drunk on homemade whisky, he told Reese that his father had told him that back in '24 they had brought up a huge block of nearly pure coal, and that on one side of the block was stamped four numbers— 6666—and that no one could explain them. Reese asked what that meant, and Tom said it was one more six than the number of the Beast. But what did *that* mean? Reese asked again. Bad place, Tom had said, as he took one swig after another, bad place.

Reese was similarly alone, though more for lack of options than for anything else. His father was struggling, working his land to the northeast of Moweaqua, and his mother was the only extra mouth he could afford to feed. So Reese was sent out on his own at sixteen, much like Tom had been, to find his way. Reese told himself he didn't mind it, that it only made sense that he would have to make a life for himself. And he believed it, most of the time.

But now the two were coming home, finding work at the Stombaugh's place to the southwest of town, out where Flatbranch Creek ran. Old Stombaugh's thrasher had up and quit on him, and hiring the team was cheaper than getting the old one fixed, and so the deal was struck, and the work was begun. It was a five-man team— there was Reese and Tom, of course; Woes, a kid Reese's age whose real name was Wozniak, though everyone shortened it because it seemed to fit his long, troubled face; Stupak, a thick, dull-headed young man whose favorite meal was spit-roast squirrel; and Fiddler, the elder of the group at about forty who everyone thought played the fiddle, but, in fact, didn't. His name was actually Fiedler, but everyone mispronounced it, and he didn't mind. He was thinking of learning how to play, he often said, if only to stop the incessant questioning from strangers. Tom, Reese, Stupak, and Woes were the muscle of the team, working the forks, while Fiddler was the feeder. The four on the ground would heave the wheat by the forkful onto a plat-form, and the feeder up top would scrape the sheaves in a bunch at a time, making sure that nothing jammed. The chaff would fill the air; the grain would spill out the other side, into a wagon, like a waterfall of gold. They worked from dawn until dusk, and had Sundays off. They were into their third day when Fiddler fell sick with the flu—nothing to take lightly since the epidemic of '22—and couldn't work the feeder platform. So Old Jules called in another man to take his place. He was a stranger, all the way from St. Louis.

Tom wasn't much for strangers. Neither was anyone else on the crew. A stranger disrupted the cadence of the job, threw everyone off in their attempts to fit in. His swing with the fork was slow, or his pace was too fast, or he talked too much, or tried to be too friendly. Anything new was a nuisance, even for a crew that had only been together for a short time, and possibly a danger. And so the men on the crew—all of them, Reese included—disliked strangers despite the fact that they had all been one at one time or another, and were themselves disliked, just as they disliked the new man before they even met him, simply because he wasn't Fiddler.

It was sunup when they all met for the first time. The fields were quiet, except for a cold wind coming up from the south. Not a good sign. Tom and Reese stood closest to the road, while Woes and Stupak sat on the platform of the thrasher, talking quietly as the machine warmed up beneath them. The stranger walked up slowly, alone, wearing only a yellow rain-slick despite the wet chill of the morning. The coat was shining, dew-touched. It looked new.

Tom nodded to the stranger as he approached, but the man in the yellow coat said nothing, having either not seen Tom or ignoring him, his face turned pointedly to the earth at his feet with every step.

"Morning," Reese said loudly. The stranger was still a few good strides away. He looked up for the first time, and it struck Reese that the man's face looked like a bird's: sharp, thin, perhaps weak. His nose was long and came to a crooked ball at its tip, and the man wore a few days worth of beard. His hair was sparse and dark, his manner the same. He nodded at Reese, and came within a few feet of him.

"You in charge here?"

"No," Tom said, and crossed his arms over his chest. "I am." This wasn't quite true, Reese thought to himself, but it was true enough. Tom was the unofficial leader of the crew, calling for position changes, breaks, and quitting time simply because the first time he did so, no one questioned his right to do it.

"What's the job?"

"Didn't Jules tell you?"

"Mr. Jagerston?"

"That's right."

"Just that you needed a man to work for a day or two."

"You him?"

"Reckon I am."

There was a quiet then, and Reese moved quickly to fill it. There was a tension in the air between Tom and the stranger, an indescribable thing, but there nonetheless, hanging in the air like an icicle waiting to fall. Reese put out his hand for the stranger. "I'm Reese. Good to have you here while Fiddler is down with flu. It's tough work with five, let alone four."

"Flu, huh?" The stranger said, taking Reese's outstretched hand weakly in his and shaking almost imperceptibly before letting loose again. "What do you need done?"

"You ever worked a thrasher before?" Tom's arms were still across his broad chest.

"Been years, but yeah."

"How long?"

"Round eight. But it was one just like that one over there, what those two is sitting on."

"Done any farming in the meantime?"

"No."

"What you been doing since?"

The stranger paused. He began to speak once, but caught himself. When he finally did answer, he spoke softly, and scratched his head absently. "I already went through the interviewing with Mr. Jagerston."

"Mr. Jagerston ain't here right now. Hell, he ain't never here. We are. We work this thing. You don't know how to work a thrasher, then you got no business being here, I don't care what the hell Jules says." Tom took a few steps toward the stranger, and the stranger took one, nearly imperceptibly, back. "So I'm going to ask you once more. What you been doing since?"

The stranger paused again, and licked his front teeth. "I had some trouble with a man."

Tom said nothing. He had gotten more information than he had expected to get, and, in the face of it, had little, immediately, to say.

"What kind of trouble?" Reese asked.

The stranger shook his head. "It's over now."

Reese looked to Tom. He was staring hard at the stranger, who, in turn, was returning the gaze with equal force. "What's your name, fella?" Tom asked one last time.

"Jacobs."

Tom nodded, as though that were all the information he needed, and turned to walk back to the thrasher without another word. Reese took one more look at Jacobs, and then followed. He could hear the stranger fall in step behind him.

The sun was starting to warm the morning, and the crows were beginning to fly through the fields, diving, snatching, and flying away again. They distributed the forks to everyone, talked to Jacobs briefly about feeding the machine, but the new man seemed impatient with the instruction, and seemed to know his way around, as he had said. So the day began, cold and terse, and warmed from there with the natural heat of work and the rising sun.

For that morning, everything was golden again. Reese looked around, first to take the position up by the feeder. It was the best view that the job offered. Down on the ground, where Tom worked most of the time, the view was little but wheat, a dizzying blur of yellow sheaf and black tine against the grey metal backdrop of the thrasher. Reese, Tom, and Stupak were supposed to take turns, but Tom rarely took his, and so Stupak and Reese traded off most of the time. Woes worked around front, watching the grain spill out the other end, making sure the chute was clear, changing the bins when they got near to full. But it was up there, perched above everything, that Reese felt the most at home. It was nothing but gold there, nothing but chaff floating in the air, coating them all like a physical glow.

Once the work got going, the day went quickly. Fiddler was gone, yes, but he would be back, and the stranger, Jacobs, seemed to know what he was doing. He fell into the rhythms that were already set, feeding the wheat into the gaping, ever-ready maw of the thrasher with a steady pace. But Fiddler was the one who usually talked while working and so his presence was most sorely missed in that respect—the job was quiet that day. Instead of talking about politics—Fiddler was always talking about Hoover's mistakes and how Roosevelt was going to usher the country and maybe the world into a better era with his New Deal and all—conversation lagged, no one saying much of anything until Stupak got on a roll about game three of the World Series. It had been over a month since the Babe had broken the tie in the top of the fifth inning by pointing to the flagpole to the right of the scoreboard in center field and then hitting the next pitch out of Wrigley.

"The beginning of the end for the Cubs," mourned Stupak. He was a baseball fan like no other, having once made a trip up to Chicago just to see a doubleheader. He had slept in a park in town and then hitched a ride back the next day. He had spent all the money he had saved, not much, but enough to live on for a week or so if a man were careful. But he had said it was worth it. He had seen his team, and it was all he wanted.

No one said much. They had all heard it before, and didn't want to encourage the same conversation to start up, not today, not now, with the day nearly spent. But Stupak was on a roll. "But there's always next year, right? I mean, the Cubs, they were good this year, real good. If they can keep that play up, maybe they can put old Ruth down next fall. Right, Jacobs? What do you say, old man?" Stupak, who by this time was taking his turn working up top next to Jacobs, slapped him on the arm as he said it, and Jacobs bridled as though someone had just insulted his mother. He didn't say anything, but glared at Stupak for a long moment before going back to work.

But Stupak wouldn't let it go. "Oh, that's right, you're from St. Louis, ain't you? Probably a Cardinals fan. Hey you guys," he called down, laughing, "You hear this? We got ourselves a Cardinal fan up here!"

This time Jacobs fully ignored him, but Tom didn't. "Give it a rest, Stupak, and get back to work. We're losing sun," he called up from the ground, shouting to be heard over the running, guttural hum of the machine.

What happened next came slowly to everyone who watched it; they would all agree on this later, in the coffee shop in Moweaqua, talking about it in hushed tones over their steaming cups. It went by so fast that no one could do anything other than watch, but slowly enough that the incident would be remembered by everyone present in intricate detail for the rest of their lives. And they promised never to talk about it. Never to forget, but never to speak of it either.

What they saw was this: Stupak, a strong boy but a boy nonetheless, perhaps made careless by his failed attempt at conversation or upset at the assumed allegiance of the stranger to the wrong baseball team, began moving with excessive force and exaggerated movements. He forked up a load of wheat and nearly threw it at Jacobs's feet. Jacobs picked it up with his fork and fed it to the thrasher as Stupak turned to get more. The rhythm was off, the pattern disrupted. When Stupak came around with another forkful of sheaves, Jacobs was just barely out of his way. Stupak was going too fast, or Jacobs too slow—there would be disagreement on this point later. Whatever the case, and due to whoever's fault, when Stupak came around to dump the wheat again, Jacobs's arm was still there.

Stupak saw the stranger's arm at the last second and tried to turn the pitchfork so as to miss him, but succeeded only in putting the leftmost tine fully through the flesh of Jacobs's forearm. He pulled it out instantly, and blood followed, dripping quickly down from wrist to hand to wheat. Without a sound, the stranger pulled his fork up, the red-stained wheat still clinging at the end, and thrust the tines directly into Stupak's throat. The boy dropped his fork, and his hands fell to his sides, and he shuddered, his body jerking violently. He never raised his hands again. The stranger let go of the fork, and Stupak crumpled off the side of the platform, falling like a shot duck, heavy and limp, on the far side of the thrasher.

Reese and Tom looked at each other for a brief second, stunned, hoping to find some retraction of what had just happened in the face of the other. When none was forthcoming, both jumped for the platform at the same time, trying to get to Jacobs, but Reese was the faster of the two. He scrambled up to the platform, and the stranger was just standing there, looking down at the body. He looked up at Reese then, and it occurred to Reese—more later, in reflection, than in the moment itself—that Jacobs's eyes were dull, like he was bored, and not angry in the least bit. His mouth was open slightly, and his lips were moving like he was trying to say some small thing, but no sound came from his throat. Reese came at him without knowing exactly what he was doing, throwing a clumsy punch. The stranger brought his arm up to block the attack and used his other to push Reese. Reese was thrown off balance, and teetered dangerously close to the open, still-chewing mouth of the thrasher, but fell instead to one side, and hit the wheel hard on the way down. Reese heard Tom bellow something guttural up above him, and, from below, something in his knee snap as his leg hit the ground at an angle; then the pain took the world away for a moment.

When Reese looked up at the thrasher again, Tom was on his feet. From his place there on the broken ground, holding his knee and trying to catch the breath that the hurt had knocked from his chest, Reese saw Tom silhouetted against the darkening sky like an angry god. Woes was close, rocking and moaning over Stupak. The boy's eyes were wide open, as was his mouth, looking for all the world like he was following a well-hit ball up in Wrigley, but his neck was all wrong, torn and bloodied, unrecognizable as something that once held voice. Tom glanced down at this, and then at Reese for an instant—less than a second, surely, but it was interminable in Reese's mind—and it was this pause that later would give Reese chills. It was a look of decision, almost of opportunity. And then Tom rushed forward at the stranger, Jacobs, who looked to be simply standing there in his yellow rain-slick, spattered as it was now in Stupak's blood, picked him up like one would a child, under the arms, and threw him right into the mouth of the feeder. Jacobs fell as though he were dead already. No clamoring for foothold, no flailing for his hands to find purchase, nothing. He simply fell into the gears and blades and teeth and went the way of the wheat. Even then, he made little sound.

Reese saw this from the ground where he lay in the blood and the dirt and the chaff. He looked over at Woes, but his head was buried in his hands. Only two men had seen it happen—Reese and Stupak—and Stupak was dead. Reese saw Tom looking down at him; sweat was dripping from his hair like rainwater. He nodded at Reese, and then looked away.

"For the love of God, turn it off!" screamed Woes. The spout was already choking with human debris, the pink of flesh, the ochre of innards, the white of bone chip. Brackish blood seeped down into the bin of grain, clumping it. Tom moved slowly but did as Woes asked, and stopped the thrasher, and it thrummed to a halt with a wet, horrifying sound.

"It's all right now," Tom said. "It's over."

Reese sat in the shadows of the hulking machine, now awash in wet crimson and dusty gold. The thrasher was a dark thing to him, with the sun serving as a backdrop, and the men around it, living and dead, moving shadows. Reese could no longer look up. All was quiet around him, except for the murmuring of men, the low hum of the machine powering down, and the sound of his own labored breathing. Reese braced himself up on the wet soil with one arm, and laid his other hand on his knee. It throbbed, and his hand could do no good for it, but Reese kept it there anyway. At least he could feel the throbbing. The rest of him was numb and cold. He thought, instead, of licorice whips and the sound of ivory balls clicking together, and how perfect that was, how wonderful, and how far from here it seemed.

Flatlander

By Linda Frantzen Carlson

I've paid my dues to the god of discomfort; I've given drug-free birth—twice. I see no need to seek out the painful and uncomfortable for pleasure. In fact, my idea of roughing it is failing to find a fancy chocolate truffle on my hotel bed pillow.

But, if you're a Coloradoan, as I am, you are expected to enjoy more primitive behaviors like camping, skiing, four-wheeling, mountain climbing, white water rafting, bear wrestling…in fact, anything roughly akin to hunting rhinos with spears. I say, what's wrong with a rousing round of croquet followed by a full-body massage?

Although, over the years, I've begrudgingly agreed to go camping on more occasions than I care to admit, it is the trip we made when I was three months pregnant with our second daughter, Traci, that has earned—in my mind—the questionable honor of most memorable. I don't remember who came up with the idea or even why I, infanticipating, went along with it, but, the plan was for us to meet at a reservoir, where—although we would be forced to sleep in tents, in sleeping bags, on the rock-hard ground—we would be camping so near to the lake, we would also have the decidedly uncamping-like luxury of getting water on our bodies.

The reservoir was several hours' drive from home in our Toyota Land Cruiser with oversized wheels and overused shocks, but my husband, Randy, reassured me it was completely reachable by paved road. This almost convinced me that pregnant or not, I might just have a bearable time. After all, should the unlikely need arise, we would still be within a day's walk of civilization.

We arrived at the reservoir about an hour later than we had planned and began slowly circling Cow Pie Campground (or something equally outdoorsy sounding), looking for what I, at least, hoped was the already set up camp of our three sets of childless friends. On the fourth time around the campground, we saw one of their trucks (four-wheel-drive, of course), rushing toward us out of the cloud of dust being kicked up by its rear tires.

Our two vehicles approached each other, stopping when driver's window aligned with driver's window.

"What's up?" my husband asked.

"We're headed for higher ground. It's too crowded here."

"How far is it?" I chanced to ask.

"Not far at all," came their mutual reply.

Thirty minutes into not far at all, we spotted the other two four-wheel-drive vehicles pulled off the side of the road in a small shaded area. They were driven by the other two childless couples of our party of nine. Strapped in a car seat in the back of *our* four-wheel-drive vehicle sat our darling twenty-three-month-old daughter Tessa. Unlike the others, we were with child (in more ways than one).

Oh, good! I thought, we're finally there!

But, au contraire! There, we weren't. We had simply stopped to risk exposing our private parts to poison ivy and, perhaps more importantly, to turn in the hubs on the four-wheel drives. So much for "completely reachable by paved road."

"How much farther?" I asked, trying to disguise the trepidation in my voice.

"Not far at all," came the chorused reply.

Randy quickly read the message behind my glare and momentarily glanced at my bulbous belly. "I'll go slow," he reassured me.

As if he had any choice in the matter.

A four-wheel-drive vehicle with oversized wheels is a wonder to behold as it traverses backcountry roads with chuckholes the size of Cincinnati. It actually seems to walk, like a grizzly, placing one tire-paw ahead of the next: front left in the ravine, right rear hanging precariously from the adjacent cliff, the other two spinning unproductively in midair.

Mile after mile, what seemed like hour upon hour. Bounce-a-da, bounce-a-da, bounce. Rock-jiggle-shake-joggle-shake. My husband wore a glazed look of primitive determination, his mouth locked in a half-smile. Our daughter in the back giggled like she'd never had so much fun, while the one in my belly felt her way around the meringue that had once been my amniotic fluid.

It was early afternoon when we arrived at the campground, but thick swarms of winged insects blocked the sun, casting shadows over the campground, mimicking twilight.

The area had been flooded by heavy spring snowmelt, which made a veritable pond of the turnoff, navigation of which was only possible by flooring one's gas pedal hard enough to reach a speed in excess of sound, propelling the vehicle into flight. This proved to be impossible for a four-wheel-drive Toyota Land Cruiser with oversized wheels. Randy gunned the gas so hard that his Frye boot might have left a print in the dirt beneath the floorboard. Tessa, still strapped in the back, bounced so hard she bit her lower lip and stopped giggling like she'd never had so much fun. And the Land Cruiser responded by leaping precisely into the center of the lagoon, mud undulating in all directions.

As soon as I saw what was happening, I frantically began rolling up my window, and although my cranking arm became little more than a blur, I wasn't fast enough.

Droplets of mud found their way into my hair and mouth and polka-dotted my face with earthen acne.

But, at last, we arrived. The Land Cruiser still cruised, the blood had stopped flowing from Tessa's lower lip, and hey, what's a bit of grunge on your face when you're camping? As far as I can tell, it's a requirement.

The next step wasn't a matter of choosing the best of several good sites upon which to pitch our dome tent. It was rather a matter of stretching the imagination far enough to envision anything vaguely resembling flat ground. The better spots had been immediately staked out by those first to conquer the sea of mud. We were the third vehicle of four in the caravan, so we didn't get the *worst* spot, or so I'm told. So much for pregnant women and children first.

It was the flies that first alerted me to the fact that something was amiss. Of course, flies are always around a campsite, but I'm talking plague here. Large in size as well as in number, these monsters droned past our heads like crop dusters.

I'm not sure how we managed to set up our tent with one hand while playing shoofly and preventing our toddler from waddling out of sight with the other, but we did. We unrolled the sleeping bags and laid them out on the floor of the tent. Then we lay down on the bags, Randy sighing contentedly, while I tried to imagine what flight of fancy would be required to perceive the ground as soft and lumpless. Looking up, I noticed the rapid fluttering of myriad wings near the dome of the tent. Randy and I had chosen a spot near a fallen tree, thinking perhaps we could use the log later as a nice perch from which to star-gaze. The head of my sleeping bag rested inside the tent, right next to the fallen tree.

I sat up. Did something smell funny, or was I imagining it? And that buzzing sound! It was so loud—and so close!

Hesitantly, I emerged from the dubious safety of our temporary digs to investigate and made my way to the section of the tent adjacent to where my head had been resting just moments before. There, just above the star-gazing log, hovered the thickest flock of flies I'd ever seen. Now and again one would nose dive to the far side of the log, then fly back up to join the airborne congregation.

I peeked over the log to see if I could determine the source of the hubbub and soon wished I hadn't. My fellow campers and I had inadvertently stumbled into the decaying remains of a poacher's paradise. Quietly decomposing on the far side of the log was the headless carcass of a stag deer. And the carnage didn't stop at our little log. Strewn throughout the grounds of our chosen weekend retreat were Bambi-like body parts. Here a head, there a leg, everywhere a hoof-hoof…

But did we leave? Did Ponce de León avoid the aging process while searching for the fountain of youth? No, he probably grew decrepit thinking, I know it's around here somewhere. It's probably not far at all. In the manner of true mountain men, we toughed it out, finding ingenious and creative ways to cohabitate with the vermin, like setting up our collapsible dining table far enough from the body parts so as not to confuse the more ravaged members with our ground beef after sunset. And, we discovered that if we stood in the very center of the campfire smoke, the flies were somewhat less of a bother.

Given such circumstances, you can stretch a four-day weekend into something near interminable. But Sunday evening finally arrived, and my filthy, smelling, sun-burned family, myself, and at least half a dozen stowaway flies finally packed our-selves back into the Toyota Land Cruiser with oversized wheels and overused shocks. We were worn out, but nevertheless touched by the experience. Let's face it, anyone who would endure such a weekend would have to be a bit touched.

Not quite a year later, we were a happy family of four. The Fourth of July was just a few weeks away when Randy got that far away look in his eyes and Tessa started giggling like she'd never had so much fun. This time I had to put my foot down. Al-though all that prepartum jostling didn't seem to have negatively affected Traci, our youngest daughter, I was a little worried about the bubbles she had suddenly begun to blow. They looked disconcertingly like meringue.

Train Going Away

By Chris Ransick

The room had looked tiny—much smaller than I remembered it. That's what struck me as I stood in the glaring sun, hands cupped to the window so I could see through the filthy glass. Dust swirled in shafts of light, marking the emptiness. The woman and her little boy had gone, along with the ratty furniture they'd scrounged from alleys and the chipped plates and cups that were always piled high in the sink.

I knew the room wasn't any smaller than it had been. It was just the unexpected absence of her and the boy that had made my life suddenly shrink. I didn't quite understand it then. Now I know all too well how that works. I've had more practice at it.

I was nineteen and a stranger in Southern California. My brother had been kind enough to let me stay at his place while I tried to earn some money. I think he understood how it was to run out of options. I'd suffered through one aimless year of college, then bailed out and went off on my first big mistake—an ill-advised adventure in eastern Wyoming. A friend had lured me there on the promise that his survey crew had regular work. He'd exaggerated. All they offered was for me to fill in a couple days a week for guys who regularly drank themselves sick in the small town bars. The high plains nights were cool, the skies deep blue and awash with more stars than I had ever seen, but I was soon more desperate than I'd been when I arrived. I never had even a hundred dollars to my name that whole summer and after listening one August night to an old guy's story of a winter he'd spent in a drafty sheep trailer, I used all my cash for a hot meal, a phone call to my brother, and a bus ticket.

This story is not about any of that. It has more to do with a woman I met in California, and her four-year-old son. Her name was Carol. She had a thick New Jersey accent and an attitude to match. She was short, barely five feet tall, with olive skin and brown eyes, and she wore her wavy brown hair in a long ponytail. We met at the Parks and Recreation district office, in a line of ragged people looking for work. It was a long wait, and eventually we started talking. I told her about my friend and his miserable survey crew, and she said she'd been to Wyoming, too, a long time ago. She said she ended up in L.A. because that was where her ancient Chevy pickup truck finally broke down. She didn't exactly say where she was headed when it happened, or where she'd come from, and I didn't ask.

After filling out the applications we smoked cigarettes out on the patch of lawn in front of the Parks Department office and then she said goodbye because she had to get back to her little boy who was home alone. I didn't expect to see her again. I'd also given up on a job with the city when a few days later I got a call that there was work mowing lawns at various parks.

The first day, when I showed up to work at the maintenance yard, I saw Carol. She was loading saplings onto a flatbed trailer when I arrived. She didn't miss a beat, as though our conversation a few days before had never really ended.

"I told them to hire you," she said with a grin. "I'm glad to see they took my advice."

"Thanks," I said. "You don't know how bad I needed this."

She gave a little laugh and shook her head. "Yes, I do," she said. "Yes, I do."

That day after work I offered to buy her a coffee. I wanted to show my appreciation. Little did I know it would get to be a habit. Soon we were going a couple times a week to a greasy spoon on Prairie Avenue, where we would share a large plate of French fries and drink a whole pot of coffee. She always stopped off at her apartment to pick up her little boy, a scruffy, quiet kid named Robbie. He had the same wavy hair and big, brown eyes, and I thought he was about the most easygoing kid I'd ever met. A lot of the time he was off in his own world, playing some kind of ongoing outer-space adventure with sugar packets and straw wrappers for space ships. Occasionally he would look up at me and smile, then go back to his game. Sometimes I would float a French fry spaceship into his little universe, expecting him to shoot his lasers and blast me to bits, but he always just sidled up to my vessel and made friends with my spacemen. Robbie liked to have a vanilla milkshake with his fries. I guessed from the way he ate it was probably his main meal each day.

An endless capacity for hot coffee was a clue about Carol. I soon learned that Carol liked to speed and I became her passenger. She often brought along to the restaurant these little white pills. The first time she offered them, I didn't hesitate, afraid I'd look like a fool. I nonchalantly took several and chased them with a swallow of coffee.

Carol gave a little laugh and poured one into her palm. "I prefer to snort them," she said, and excused herself to go to the restroom. I hadn't expected that.

The next morning, my hands were still jittery. I hadn't slept at all.

Although I became her friend, we weren't lovers. That seems important to mention, though I'm not sure why. I just remember that I spent a lot of my free time that autumn with her and Robbie, and for the first time in a while, I was content. I had a bit of money from the lawn mowing job and could pay my brother for food and rent. He never asked for it, but I would put money on the kitchen table after payday and he accepted the gesture.

Sometimes after our "meals," Carol, Robbie, and I would walk across the tracks—I mean this literally—to her shabby apartment. We'd talk late into the night, listening to the radio and watching out the window as the occasional freight train would lumber past. We'd have a couple glasses of cheap wine if we had enough money, and more of the little white pills from her endless supply, and Robbie would play with his simple toys: plastic margarine tubs, a branch from a dead bush out front, and his favorite, a filthy, tattered stuffed animal. Carol would tell stories in her Jersey accent and when she laughed, I could see that laughing didn't chase the dark circles from under her eyes. But I liked it when she laughed, and I felt at ease there on the dirty carpet, where we sat for lack of any chairs. Even after I'd helped her to scrounge a couple of battered chairs from the alley nearby, we'd still sit on the carpet.

"You know," she told me one time, "I can't figure out why you hang around here. I mean, how old are you?"

"I'll be twenty soon," I said.

"Why aren't you out chasing down girls and getting your share of pussy, like most of the other guys your age?" As she said this, she blew a stream of cigarette smoke in my direction. I wasn't used to women talking like this, though it was common enough among guys. But Carol was different from any woman I'd ever known and that's what I liked about her.

I shrugged. "I don't like chasing," I said. "Besides, there's no hurry."

"Oh, there will be," she said. "But that still doesn't explain what you're doing here."

I realized she actually wanted some kind of honest answer. I looked around the room a moment, took another swig from the bottle of wine. "I guess I just like hanging around with Robbie. Great kid, you know."

She smiled, looked over at her son, then back at me. She was about to say something, but didn't.

· ——— ·

My brother's place was in Carson. That's not one of the pampered beach cities. It's a gritty place inside the smog belt where the heavy, ochre air settles in on hot days, where the aging strip malls are interspersed with dense rows of shabby stucco dwellings, ringed by palm trees all slouched and grey with disease. Carol's neighborhood was tucked behind an industrial park that was still served by a rail spur, the kind of place where every ground level window has iron bars and where harried looking store owners pull accordion gates across the entrances to their graffiti-laced stores each evening.

We had been hanging around together for almost two months when I showed up unexpectedly one Saturday at her place. She opened the door, looking very tense, and waved me in, a cigarette in her hand. Robbie was sitting on the back porch steps—I could see him through the open screen door.

A man was leaning against the kitchen sink, his powerful arms and stained overalls suggesting he worked around heavy machinery. To my surprise, he nodded at me. I took a seat on a dilapidated couch, which hadn't been there before, the thought running through my head that I shouldn't be in that precise spot at that particular moment. Don't stay long, I told myself, just long enough to keep from looking like an idiot—but it was already too late for that.

Carol ignored me for the moment and went over to talk with this fellow, their voices hushed, their words nothing I could make out. I wasn't really trying to hear them, and after it went on for a few moments, I got up and walked toward the door.

"Wait," Carol said, "don't leave."

I explained that I had just stopped in on my way home, which was a lie, and that I had to get going, which was also a lie because I had nowhere to go but back to my brother's apartment.

"Wait," she said again, this time more urgently. The man was still standing where he had been before, his arms crossed over his chest and his face expressionless. I told Carol I'd have a smoke out on the porch, and she tossed me the pack that was on the counter.

It just so happened that as I stepped outside, a freight train was coming from a short distance off and making its slow way down the center strip that ran the length of the street. I lit one of the cigarettes and watched the train's slow advance, then stepped out into the street and moved toward the tracks. The train finally crossed the spot a few yards away from where I stood and I found myself wondering what was in the dusty cars, screeching and lurching past.

Then, suddenly, there was somebody beside me.

It was the man from Carol's apartment. He nodded at me again—really just a jutting of the chin that some guys use as a greeting—and he indicated the cigarettes. I handed him the pack, he took one out, and then with a deft shake of his wrist set another cigarette protruding out of the pack. I figured I had better take it, and I did. He stowed the pack in the breast pocket of his overalls.

So there I was smoking, which I rarely did before meeting Carol, alongside a man I'd never met and about whom I knew little. A strange worry knotted in my gut, nothing I'd ever felt before. Then an even stranger thing happened.

"I'm Robbie's father," the man said above the rumble of the box cars. His voice was calm and matter-of-fact, and I thought I saw him smile as he said it. "I came round because tomorrow's his birthday. I try to come around on his birthday."

Now it was my turn to nod. I took a drag on my cigarette and tried to make myself look older, which was no use. But he didn't show any contempt and I realized he hadn't come out to threaten me, as I had feared.

"You known Carol long?" he asked.

"Not really," I said. "A couple of months. I met her at work."

He nodded again, then said, "Robbie doesn't much like the fact that she's gone some days, but it's a good thing that she's found work."

"Robbie's a good kid," I said.

The man nodded. "He's a good kid," he said.

I don't know what made me say it, but the words escaped before I could rein them in. "I try to be nice to Robbie," I said.

It was true. A week earlier I had brought him an old baseball glove I'd found at my brother's house, though I didn't think far enough ahead to bring a ball. When I gave it to Robbie, he didn't know what it was. I had to put it on his hand, which looked so small in the mitt that I immediately felt stupid for bringing it. I got an orange from the counter and used it as a ball, showing him how to catch a short toss. He learned quickly and we only stopped when the orange split and started oozing. Carol couldn't hide her amusement.

I told the man about the baseball glove although I wasn't so sure I should.

"That's good," the man said. "He's old enough now he ought to learn to catch."

The pause filled the night air between us as we stood shoulder to shoulder, and without looking at the man, I said, "You know, I just think I ought to say about Carol and me, it's not what you might think."

The man took a long drag on his cigarette and shook his head slowly from side to side. "That's no matter to me," he said. "I got a woman of my own down in Long Beach, and a baby boy."

I nodded. I could see, down the track, the last car on the train. We both watched it grind slowly toward us. "I wonder what's in these train cars," I said as the last one reached the spot where we were standing.

He paused while it receded, shook his head again. "Nothing in those cars," he said. "That's how you know they're leaving."

We finished our cigarettes in silence. He nodded once more toward me, went to his car, a restored late 60s model Impala, and drove off along the avenue, the street lamps glowing orange overhead.

It wasn't long afterward when I arrived at work one morning and found the manager waiting to talk with me. He'd noticed that Carol and I often left work together and had probably assumed I'd know why she hadn't shown up at work the last couple of days.

"You have any idea where she is?" he asked. "She's got no telephone so I can't check up with her. Is she sick or something, or maybe the kid?"

"I don't know," I told him.

He looked at me a long moment. "If you happen to talk with her, let her know I've got a list as long as doomsday of people that want the job and I won't hold it for her past Friday. You tell her that."

I decided I would check in on Carol after work. It was a long day. My jeans and sneakers were stained green and my ears were ringing from hours behind the mower. On my way to Carol's place I stopped at a liquor store where I knew the owner, a bent old man who was mostly deaf, would sell me a bottle of wine so long as I bought a sandwich. The store was just down the street from Carol's apartment. I remember thinking to myself as I crossed the train tracks that if I didn't know better, I would have guessed no train had ridden those rails in decades.

When I got to Carol's place, I knocked. No answer. I knocked again, louder this time, hoping she was just asleep.

I finally turned to go and saw the sun glint off the window where the ragged drapes had been slightly pulled back. I turned back and when I cupped my hands to the window and peered inside, I could see the place was empty.

In the Slatted Light

By A. Rooney

1.

The flight arrives early and I'm late by twenty minutes. I'm at the gate, Frances is already at the baggage carousel. First thing she says is "Where have you been?" I try to tell her about the traffic on I-70 and Marty Koin's funeral and she says, "Watch my bag, I really have to go to the ladies' room."

In the car she tells me about the Picasso show in Manhattan, seeing Spike Lee on the Jersey shore, going up to Harlem with her friends. But I don't especially want to talk about any of these things.

"Do you like these new shoes?" she says. They're open in the back and look like expensive clogs. I say I like them. I want to tell her about Marty, the get together at the Eighth after the funeral, and the fact that we never reconciled. We were friends, but somehow we let our relationship with Roberta interrupt that and we could never quite get back to fixing it.

"Let's go someplace good to eat," she says.

"Okay," I say, "but first let's take a look at a trailer."

"What kind of trailer?"

I tell her about a camping trailer I called on in the paper, and that I've been thinking about getting one.

"You mean like those little things, like retired people pull behind their cars?"

"Yeah, so we can go up into the mountains even when it's cold and we don't have to sleep on the ground."

"We don't sleep on the ground now anyway."

"Yeah, but this way we save on motels and ski condos."

"No way am I sleeping in some little trailer when it's snowing outside."

We drive through the suburbs southeast of Denver, talk about Frances' trip, her friends, the things she did. I think of Marty the whole time and want Frances to ask about him or the funeral or the relationship. When she doesn't, I put it aside and concentrate on finding the address I'm searching for. I finally locate it and get out to look at the trailer while Frances stays in the car.

I talk to the woman with the trailer about pull weight, tongue weight, and she tells me that she and her husband used to go all over in it, even when it was snowing.

"But now that he's dead," she says, "I don't want to use it anymore, I'm going to live with my daughter."

I like the trailer, can see myself beside a stream in northern New Mexico, reading novels, listening to the radio.

"My husband took excellent care of the trailer," she says, "the tires are almost new."

I ask how old the trailer is and if they used it a lot.

"We used it a lot more after he retired," she says, "in fact, we were down by Nogales in the trailer when he died. Had a coronary, just like that."

"You didn't have any warning, no stomachache, no chest pain?" I say.

"Nope," the woman says, "he'd just finished a bowl of Cream of Wheat and was reading the paper. He was sitting outside under the awning, I was inside cleaning up. I heard him say, 'Hon, Hon,' and then he was gone."

"That's too bad," I say, "sorry about your loss."

"We had some good times in this trailer. He would have died ten years ago if we hadn't had it."

I get out my checkbook, go over to the car to talk with Frances. She rolls the window down just a few inches.

"What?" she says.

"I think I'd like to buy it."

"What are we gonna do with a trailer like that?"

"Go places, do things, see some country."

"In a little thing like that?"

"Yeah, I'm ready to do some traveling, some exploring."

"You're not getting me to sleep in that thing when it's cold. And if you think I'm gonna be doing a lot of cooking and making pancakes forget about it."

I look to the west at the lightly dusted Rockies, am not sure what to do. I put my checkbook away and tell the woman I'll have to think about it, maybe call her back. At dinner we eat at Carmen's on Penn, order pasta in an arrabiata sauce with a seafood medley. Frances picks the mussels and squid out. While she talks about going to see Harold Melvin at the Apollo, I'm traveling. Baja and up the Alaska coast. The Black Hills. The Trans-Can. The Boundary Waters. Maine. Chesapeake Bay. The Keys. The Gulf. Mardi Gras.

"Are you listening?" Frances says.

"Yeah," I say, "I'm listening."

A note from my tenant is taped to the door when I get home:

Low, abt the rnt. I got a hndrd cash in my pockt I could give you but thot youd prob want it all at one time. The other I can hve to you no latr than Thurs. With the rain and evthg, I hvnt been able to work outerdrs much and am a little slow with my bills this mo.

In rgrds to your note Iam tryng to get that car movd but the wrench says he wont be ready for it untl the wknd. Thats where all of my money has ben going, to get a new engin, the other hvg a warpd head as you know. The mech says he can do it for 200 cash and I got 400 this wk so that leaves a 100 for me and a 100 for rent.

Which I know is short by 325 and I will pay the remndr for sures next Sat, or Sun at the outside latst. Which remnds me. The drip in the ktchn sink has got steadier and kept me up all of one nite the other nite. I even tryd leavg a spunge in the sink but aftr awhile that didnt do nogood nowise. And the nhbrs upstairs have been going at it again. Draging and movg.

I hve tried to be nice about it, but they bein late people and me a early bird we hve had some words. He is still Greek as you know and she is somethig else. But they still hve that German car. Ervin.

2.

We leave the meeting at the church, Ray and I, and get into my car. The group put the final touches on the annual Spring Equinox celebration. In five days dozens of men will gather in the mountains west of Denver.

"This will be good," Ray says, "we'll have a big bonfire every night, dance, drum, share some truth, smoke some herb."

"I thought we weren't supposed to bring any drugs," I say and feel myself tensing. After my conviction I get paranoid whenever it's around.

"Low, we just don't want people bringing any of the hard stuff, the heavy shit. I know you're not into that anymore but nothing wrong with a little doob on special occasions."

In the car on the way to the Eighth I tell Ray about Frances' trip and the trailer and then he reads the back of the weekly newspaper out loud.

"Guaranteed acne treatment. Instant cash. Walk-in massage. Genital herpes study. Nose, tongue, whatever pierced while you wait. What's the alternative?"

"To what?"

"To getting your piercings done while you wait?"

"Leave your parts, I guess, the Van Gogh approach."

Ray continues.

"Herbalife. Elegant—discreet. Cars from $500. Prevent photo radar. Slim and busty. Voodoo tattoo."

I wonder if he'll read every headline aloud. It's one of his most irritating traits, that and changing the stations on the car radio.

"Adopt-a-pet. Men's spa. Have you been injured?"

"Ray, Ray," I say.

"What?"

"Didn't you put an ad in there, in the personals, before you met your new girlfriend?"

"Yeah."

"What did it say?"

"Did a little checking first and found some things out."

"Like what things?"

"It's code, they're all in code."

"You mean like SBF-DWM?"

"No, and that's hardly code anymore. Know what it means in an ad when it says a guy's laid back?"

"I don't know, maybe he's not into the whole corporate scene or the SUV thing anymore."

"It's a carryover. Means he doesn't have good hygiene and smokes weed on the weekends. And what's your guess when it says entrepreneur or consultant?"

"Hard to say, maybe he operates one of those hot dog carts downtown."

"Close. He's out of work, collecting the last of his unemployment and needs a woman to help out with the rent."

"How'd you come up with these things, Ray?"

"Took me a while, man. Asked a lot of questions, called people up, put two and two together. So what do you think it means when the guy says he's just returned from abroad?"

"I don't know. Is that a pun?"

"No, serious."

"He got fired from a job overseas?"

"Nah, means the guy was in prison, no offense, but he's probably a convicted felon. And when he says he's mentally stable, what would you make of that?"

"Maybe it means his ex-wife or his last girlfriend was bipolar, and he's just putting it out there so he doesn't repeat."

"I like that, but more than likely, the guy's just telling people he's mentally stable now, thanks to the lithium."

I start to ask another question and Ray interrupts.

"Did I tell you about June and *Love to Meet a 41 Reg*?"

"No, whatever *Love to Meet a 41 Reg* means."

"You know I got this thing for nice sports coats, right?"

"Yeah, I've seen your wardrobe."

"Well, there was an ad in the paper that said this woman's husband died and left her a closet full of these really expensive sport coats, all forty-one regular. And she'd been in mourning for a couple years and she was ready to spread her wings again."

"Was that last part code for something?"

"Yeah," Ray says. "When I tell you how she was dressed the first night you'll know for what. Anyway, in the ad she said all that trash about walking in the moonlight, laughing together, and listening to jazz and that she wanted a special man to wear the coats again."

"So what did you do?"

"I called the Loveline and left her a message that I was a forty-one regular and that I was a real coat guy."

"And she called you back?"

"Couple hours later. 'Do you want to come to dinner,' she said, 'I'll cook something special, what do you like, I'm a gourmet cook.' 'Anything,' I said, 'make your favorite dish. Tell me a little about the coats, I'm curious.' 'My husband only bought the finest wool, cashmere, and silk,' she said, 'the finest.' 'Sounds like he had good taste,' I said, 'must have been hard losing him.' 'He'd become an intolerable asshole,' she said, 'but he knew coats and material. I'm very much looking forward to meeting you, Ray,' she said, 'see you Saturday.'

"When I got to her house she was wearing this filmy top," Ray says, "and she had on perfume that was like an aphrodisiac."

With his eyes closed he talks about running his hands over the expensive coats in the closet, trying on one after the other, and the incredible dinner. Something about it, the richness, the sexuality, triggers a memory of the time I was in L.A., visiting my friend Helene the nurse, smoking hash on Balboa Pier. It was springtime, right at sunset.

"Let's go over to my friend's house," Helene says, "do some mushrooms."

The friend is also a nurse but she's obese, raises Pomeranians, and there are dogs and puppies everywhere. The friend has a mushroom punch and the three of us drink it. Helene goes into the back bedroom, calls out to me a few minutes later. She's lying naked on an antique four-poster, canopy and gauzy curtains around it. She's lathered herself in scented oil. I take off my clothes and the other one comes in. She's wearing a thick terrycloth robe, open in the front. She begins to dance a little, slides the robe off.

"Is it okay if Sylvie stays?" Helene says.

"So I stay," Ray is saying, "and I leave in the morning after breakfast. She's got two expensive cars sitting in the garage and she wants me to drive one home."

I've thought about that night in Balboa often, about the sheer curtains, about the two of us applying oil to Sylvie's ample skin, about seeing Sylvie fondle herself and shuffledance around us as we make slow mushroom love on the big bed. It's hard to remember actually being there, doing that. It doesn't seem wild or exciting now, only indulgent and immature, even somewhat revulsive.

"So, what about the coats?" I say absently, rebreathing Sylvie's oiled flesh.

"Man, without a doubt the finest material I've ever seen. She gave me a beautiful chocolate cashmere to take with me."

"What do you think, Ray, you going to keep seeing her?"

"She started calling me sweetheart the first night. 'Sweetheart we could go on trips,' she said, 'and I'll pay for everything.' She said she had money and she didn't mind taking care of me."

"That scare you?"

"Yeah," Ray says, "a little."

3.

Ray and I sit and talk with James as he mixes drinks and pours beer. James stops to wash glasses and tells us his neighbor has seen foxes on their block.

"Yeah, she said there was a pair of them."

"Where do they live?" Ray says. "I've never seen anything like that over where I am."

"I don't know," James says, "under houses, in culverts, at the country club. This is my neighbor the old beautician and while she was watching them they caught and ate a damn cat, pulled it apart, then buried it in somebody's garden."

As James and Ray talk I put my hand on the bar and look around at the interior of the place I've spent part of my adult life. The bar was obviously built in mismatched stages, in a mix of oak and cherry. The floor is covered with small black and white tile and there's a hodgepodge of signs, postcards, and old menus on the walls, but no motif to speak of. When we first sat down James talked about the day he and Leo took over from the original owner, Mrs. Heck, and apparently it's the anniversary of that day.

The conversation shifts when James waits on someone else and Ray asks if I've heard from my sister, Deanne.

"Two, three weeks," I say.

"How's she doing in New York?"

"Working too hard on that sitcom, making lots of money, getting tired of the city."

Ray reminds me he has always had a thing for Deanne, even when she was just fourteen, and that she can make him laugh harder than anybody he knows. I remember watching Ray at twenty-one with her, wondering on a few occasions if I was going to have to intervene.

"If she still liked boys, you might have a chance," I say.

"Are she and that actress currently living together?"

"Actress-director, and it sounds like they're about to end it. How's your new lady friend with the coats?"

"You mean June? She's all right. I just learned she lived in a commune for a long time near Gardner."

"The Libre commune? I wonder if she was in their band?"

"She didn't say anything about that, only that that's where she met her husband, the coat meister."

"What did he do?"

"He was an attorney. Living out in Gardner he got to know a lot about water law and later became a big shot water attorney."

"What happened to him?"

"Cancer of the liver, too much dope."

"I probably met the guy, probably her too, one of the times I went down to Libre to buy drugs."

"Is that where you were getting all that stuff? Man, for a while you had so much dope in your house."

"I was getting it everywhere. When I'd run out, Libre would always have more."

"Honestly, I didn't think you were gonna make it for a while. I didn't think you were gonna be able to stop."

"I didn't want to stop. I liked it. I still have dope dreams. Unfortunately I probably wouldn't have stopped if I hadn't gotten busted."

"Yeah, getting busted will do that. Low, ever see Linnie any more, ever wonder about her?"

"I saw her at King Soopers a few months ago. She was with her husband and their little girl. She looked pretty good."

"How old is their kid now?"

"She's ten or eleven. Real pretty little girl."

"Who did she marry?"

"Tomas, you know him. Big guy, used to come in here once in a while. Had brothers."

"Yeah, I sorta remember him. Had real white teeth?"

"That's him. All of them had teeth like that."

"Ever wonder what happened to the baby?"

"Not a day goes by I don't think about him. He'd be almost thirty now. Probably has kids of his own. My mother wanted to keep him, raise him, I don't know if you knew that. I tried to talk Linnie into an abortion but her family wouldn't let her."

"You were fucked up, Low. I'm your friend, I can tell you. You lost your teaching job and Linnie and the baby. You were fucked up then."

"I know. I know."

I shake my head at Ray's comment, catch a glimpse of myself being stopped on the highway, the arrest and trial, the years in prison detox, the humiliation of it all.

"I was thinking the other day," Ray says, "remember the time after Kent State we had that demonstration and stormed the president's office?"

"What made you think of that?"

"Something on TV, I don't know, them arresting that woman who was a Weatherman. It just came to me."

"What I remember most about that day is I was never so scared in my life."

"What were you scared of, the cops coming and knocking all of us on the head?"

"I was afraid you and the crowd were going to drag old Dr. Vickers out and hurt him, maybe kill him, Ray."

"Nah, some of us had decided we were going to kick him out of his office, maybe occupy the building."

"It started to get ugly, you had his arm behind his back. The criminals of the college were there and it became a mob. I could see the whole thing unfolding."

"That why you took over? I never said anything before but I've always wondered about that."

"I saw the look on those guys' faces, like they were at the coliseum, and it scared me. We were there to make a statement, not to have a public hanging. I didn't want to go to jail for something stupid like that."

Ray and I met at freshman orientation and we've been friends ever since. He managed to get a job with a corporation and keep it over the years. While I was in prison he visited me every week, brought books. He's a little bit of a troublemaker himself, but he's got a good heart.

"Today I tried to park as close to the Safeway as I could," Ray says. "I drink only decaf now. I hold the handrail when I use the stairs. I have to get up in the middle of the night to take a leak. I haven't had a shot of tequila in years. June wanted to fuck twice in one night and I had to tell her to wait. What's happening, Low?"

"What's happening is we woke up and discovered we're not really revolutionaries or giant killers or lover boys and we're not going to be. We discovered if we didn't hurry we'd die without owning any real estate and that we didn't have any choice except to get on the train and stay on."

"You still write those little stories, Low?"

"Yeah, once in a while."

"Ever send any out?"

"I sent a bunch out when I got out of Ft. Logan, a couple recently, but I haven't tried real hard. They're just little sketches, not big stories."

"Let me read them sometime. I think the only ones you ever showed me were the couple about the Eighth."

"Yeah," I say, "I did a few of those."

"I'd like to see those stories, Low, really."

4.

My mother, Dorothy, ticks at the back door with her fingernail. I can see her face through the glass and open the door. She wants to know if I'll help her look for Arnie.

"He's gone," she says, "and his asthma is back. You haven't seen him, have you?"

"No, I haven't seen him," I say, "but we can go look for him if you want."

"I hope he comes back," she says, "and no dog eats him."

We walk around our block completely and an adjacent one, but no Arnie. I tell my mother we can make signs and post them in the neighborhood, see if that helps. She likes that idea.

When we get back Dorothy gets a chair, puts it by the sink. It's the first Friday, the day I do my mother's hair, and she lays a coloring pouch on the counter. As we talk, I wet it with the sprayer, massage her scalp. My father used to wash and color her hair, even after he started to get sick. After he died she asked me to do it. Initially I balked, but now we use it as a time to catch up.

My mother lives in one of my apartments. A few years ago she sold the house, didn't want to take care of anything but her cat Arnie. She wanted to do things with her friends, didn't want to be tied down, so I rented her one of my vacant units. I refuse to let her pay so she cleans my place, does the laundry, takes care of the property if I go away. I tell her about seeing Ray at the Eighth the night before, and about Marty's funeral, and she tells me about one of the tenants, Gail.

"She'll be thirty-seven tomorrow. Poor thing. No boyfriend, no buddies, just her plants. Somebody ought to take her out this weekend, help her celebrate."

"That would be a nice thing for somebody to do," I say, squeezing the water out of her hair.

"I told her you were thinking of taking her out for a drink," Dorothy says.

"Mom," I say stepping back, "what did you say that for? She's thirty-seven, I'm fifty-three and I already have a girlfriend."

"You can't take her for a drink or two? Maybe down at that place you go, I'll even pay."

"Mom, that's not it. I just don't want to go through the hassle, I'm not interested. She's a tenant."

"You can't treat another human decent on her birthday? What about all those things you've said about human rights?"

"Mom, what does this have to do with human rights?"

"She's a nice girl, a pretty girl, and you could do somebody a favor once in a while. I hope if any of my children are ever alone on their birthdays that someone would buy them a drink or a little something to eat. Something."

"Okay, Mom, I'll talk to her."

"How's Frances?"

"I take her over in the morning tomorrow."

"They do it right there in the office?"

"Yeah, a laser."

"That was what her mother had, wasn't it?"

"Yeah, same thing. That's why she's so worried. They're afraid it'll spread, like her mother's."

5.

Gail and I stop at the Eighth for a drink and she asks about the Spring Equinox celebration, I told her about it on the way over. I'm still not that enthused about taking my tenant out and I can feel I'm slightly distracted. I chose the Eighth just to make the evening as public as possible.

"How many men total?" Gail says.

"Fifty or so," I say.

"And you're dancing and singing around a campfire?"

"More like a bonfire."

"And some have their clothes off?"

"Yeah, maybe a couple dozen, or their shirts or shoes."

"Were you one of the ones with your clothes off?"

"Still too cold for me. I had shorts and a sweatshirt on."

"What's it like?"

"What?"

"That many naked men dancing around?"

"The camaraderie was good, the fellowship. And it was great being outside under the stars, next to the fire."

"I just think about all those penises bobbing around."

"Yeah," I say, a little surprised at her comment, "every kind imaginable."

"Didn't you wonder if some of them, do you think some of those men were gay?"

"Yeah, probably, a few, but it wasn't a big deal. Nobody paid any attention to that."

We've been here ten or fifteen minutes and I've already begun looking at my watch. I feel bad but I'm hoping someone will come over and sit with us and I can introduce them to Gail.

"So, did your mother make you do this, ask me out for my birthday?"

"Oh, she said something, but I thought maybe you could use the company, especially today. And I take my tenants out every once in a while anyway just to be nice."

"Whatever the reason, I appreciate it."

"You told me when you moved in but I forget, where do you work?"

"US West."

"Probably not as an operator, though."

"I started as an operator but they have almost no operators anymore and they're all located someplace else. I work in the Business Acquisition Center."

"You go out and acquire more business for the company?"

"I write proposals. I sit at my desk and write hundreds of proposals every year."

"That could be interesting."

"It's stupid work, it's a stupid company, and I feel stupid doing it."

"Probably pays well."

"If it wasn't for the pay and the benefits I'd rather work almost anywhere else, including temping or the Post Office, even Sears."

I watch Gail when she gets up to go to the ladies' room. She has the kind of orange hair and large freckles that people find humorous. Her teeth are small, like corn nibblets, with big spaces between. Her hands are thin, fingernails trimmed short. She's not unattractive, I think, but there's an unfortunateness about her.

"It's funny," Gail says, "we live in the same building but all we know about each other is just that I rent apartment six and you're the landlord. We're in the same solar system but we have different orbits."

"Yeah," I say nodding, trying to think of something appropriate to say. "I wonder what that says about us, about our society."

"Are you married?" she says. "Do you have kids somewhere?"

"Not married," I say, "and I have one but it's a long story."

"What do you see when you see me?" Gail says. "You were looking at me."

I'm not sure how to respond, Gail's hands are trembling slightly. I take a deep breath. "Everything okay, you doing alright?"

"No," Gail says, "not really."

"What's up, why not, if you don't mind my asking?"

"I thought at thirty-seven it would be different."

Her eyes well with tears and she bites her lip. She cups her drink tightly with her hands.

"You don't have to do this," I say, "we can go if you like."

"No, no, that's okay. I guess I need to talk about it. I've gotten older but I don't see that I'm any different than when I was seventeen."

"What did you think would happen? What were you expecting?"

"I wanted to know more, I wanted to do something, I wanted to be more comfortable with myself, with who I am as a woman."

"Isn't there anything you enjoy, anything that turns you on?"

"You remember last summer when I started the garden?"

"Yeah, it was a pretty good garden for a while. What happened?"

"Every day I watered and weeded, and I was really looking forward to the tomatoes."

"You had a bunch of different kinds, I noticed."

"I researched them all winter: Brandywines, Burbank Reds, Yellow Pears, Cherokee Purples, Jubilees. I had starters in all my windows. In June, when it was time, I was ready. I watched them get bigger and I sprayed and knocked the aphids off every couple of days. I checked on them first thing in the morning and in the evening when I got home. I liked sitting in my chair at night, watering."

"So what happened? I noticed you quit watering."

"When the tomatoes were just about ready, every night when I would go to pick them somebody had gotten there before me. At first I thought it was one of the other tenants or that guy Ervin and it made me so mad. I watched out the window one whole day and night and I found out."

"Who was it?"

"This big black Lab from somewhere in the neighborhood would jump the fence, go right to my tomatoes, and eat the ripe ones."

"A dog ate your tomatoes, are you sure?"

"If I went in for two seconds he would be there and the tomatoes would be gone when I came out. It was like he was waiting, lurking."

"You should have said something, maybe we could have put a fence up or something around the tomatoes."

"I took an afternoon off once and put my chair out there. I had the broom in one hand and the hose in the other. I dozed off as it got later and dreamed about fields of tomatoes, every kind, little tomatoes, big tomatoes, green, red, purple, yellow, white, and they were all mine. I grew every one of them. I was the tomato lady. And then I saw them coming, this big pack of black Labs, hundreds of them, sweeping over the field, eating every tomato right off the vine. I couldn't stop them. When I awoke, the Lab was standing there with a ripe yellow tomato in his mouth, grinning.

"Wait, a dog actually came into the yard and had a tomato in his mouth?"

"Yes, and when I screamed he jumped the fence. I gave up after that, just quit watering, and I never got to eat one friggin tomato. Seems like anything I really get into, anything I really enjoy, just goes to hell."

I'm not sure what to say that would be helpful and it seems like Gail needs a little help.

"Did the dog ever come back?"

"I don't know, I never paid any more attention."

After the evening is over, when I've walked Gail back to her apartment, I wonder what it would be like to be in that kind of pain again. And then I revisit something that comes up from time to time—the idea of starting over, with a family, but in other ways, too.

6.

Frances and I sit at her kitchen table drinking coffee, eating toast. She is explaining that two menstrual periods in a month are called blue moon periods and she hopes it's all right that she didn't feel like having sex last night. I remember hearing a story on NPR about the fallacy of the blue moon.

"No big deal, Frances," I say, "there will be plenty of other times."

"The early call was my dad about my grandfather," Frances says about the call that woke us. "He found him under his bed, he'd had a heart attack."

"How did he get there, did R.O. say?"

"He doesn't know, maybe he fell or maybe he was sleeping there for some reason. He was starting to lose it, he was strange anyway."

"Did he have his slippers on?"

"What does that have to do with anything?"

"Maybe he crawled under the bed to get his slippers and he had the heart attack while he was there."

"Maybe, but he was fully dressed, with his good pants on."

"Lots of old guys wear their slippers around all the time, their regular shoes hurt their feet."

"Anyway, he's dead and having my period is a good sign for now."

"You going to the memorial service and the funeral?"

"Nah, that was the one that tried that funny business. There'll be a little thing at church on Sunday, I'll go to that."

"Frances," I say, "ever wish you'd had kids, ever wonder what that would've been like?"

"I thought about it a lot when I was a young woman and wondered if every man I met would be the father of my children. Walter never wanted to have any and he wouldn't have made a good father anyway. Then after we got divorced it just got further and further along and finally I gave up. Have you been thinking about kids, Lowell? Did having a drink with your tenant make you think of that?"

"Yeah, a little, but it's something that comes up every so often anyway, and if it doesn't, my mother brings it up."

Frances asks if I want to take a shower with her. I smile. She takes her pajamas off at the table, walks past me to the bathroom, starts the water. I watch her take her glasses off, pin her hair up, watch the profile of her small round breasts as she lifts her arms. I watch her watching herself in the mirror, admire her slender brown cheeks, join her in the shower. We hold each other in the hot water. I kiss her neck, nipples, and belly. Frances stops me, says, "Let me do this for you," and puts my penis in her mouth until I come. We wash each other with soap after and say nothing.

When we're drying off Frances rubs tiger balm on her joints and laughs, says "Remember the time in Chimayo when the car broke down?"

"I try not to," I say.

We had driven to the Santuario de Chimayo in New Mexico because Frances wanted to try the holy water and miracle dirt on her arthritis. It was only supposed to be overnight but the Taurus broke down while we were there. I sent Frances back to Denver on the bus after three days. I worried we were doing more than being short with each other.

The bed and breakfast we were staying at was too hot. We had to walk everywhere because we didn't have a car. The only restaurants besides the bed and breakfast were a bad Mexican food place and a Loaf-n-Dash. The local transmission guy, Temio, could only work on the car at night because of the heat and his thyroid condition.

After Frances left, I began sitting in the shade outside the Santuario to read and give myself something to do. One day when I'd tired of being outside, I knelt at a pew inside the church. Almost immediately I was overcome with emotion. Pictures of a lost son at every age flooded my mind. I was filled with inconsolable remorse. For a time I couldn't move.

People came to the Santuario on homemade crutches, with rosary beads in one hand, scapulas around their necks, and holding photos of dead relatives. They came in search of something and took plastic containers of the miracle dirt away with them. I stayed late one evening, watched the priest replace the dirt. We began to talk.

"I've noticed people tack notes up in the church addressed to God," I said, "why is that?"

"Faith," the priest said, "and the joy of knowing they are communicating directly with the Almighty."

"If God is truly omniscient why would they have to write notes to him?"

"Though God indeed knows all, we get weak and need reassurances that He hears our prayers and supplications. He knows that we are weak and accepts and loves us for it nevertheless."

"Maybe he isn't an all-knowing God, maybe he only knows a few things pretty well and needs to be alerted to the rest with notes in a shrine."

The priest was amused. "I have seen you here kneeling and in prayer. Have you left notes of your own?"

"Yes," I said.

"To God?" he said.

"To a boy," I said.

"Are you Catholic?" he said.

"No, Church of Christ as a kid, nothing now."

"Why are you here?"

"Today I'm praying that my transmission will be fixed soon, Father."

"Where is your car?"

"At Temio's garage."

"You are in the right place," the priest said.

The next day Temio came to the bed and breakfast, got me at three in the afternoon, and drove the two of us into Espanola for parts. Temio couldn't get credit and I had to buy everything with cash. On the way back he bought three quarts of beer with money he borrowed from me. We stopped again at a paint and body shop. Inside Temio lit up a joint with his friends, offered me a hit while they drank the beer. Two customized cars sat in the bays: One a glossy black '60 Chevy with Jesus on the hood wearing a crown of thorns. The other a candy-apple '49 Ford with a nude mermaid painted on the trunk. Two days later the transmission was done.

I paid for the car and took a big container of dirt for Frances with me. Outside Walsenburg, Colorado, the transmission slipped going up a hill, then quit. I took the plates off, walked into town for a six-pack, and caught the next bus to Denver.

7.

Frances and I ride the light rail, it's early evening. We're going downtown to see friends in *The Tempest* in a small theatre, maybe stop at the Eighth after. In the west, the sinking sun turns the mountains crimson, cold blue. Headlights come on and below are warehouses, junkyards. On a street we pass over, a man sits on the hood of a black car, yellow cat next to him, and drinks a bottle of beer.

As the train jostles along, I think about my visit Friday to the Denver Vital Statistics office at the City & County Building and the child Linnie gave up for adoption. Vital Statistics didn't have the records, wouldn't legally have been able to show them to me. Linnie was at Florence Crittenden, then used an agency. She sent me a note later; Davis, after her mother's side. I've wanted to call him or make contact after all these years, see how things are. Don't know what I'd do after that. Yeah, let's get to know each other, go to a ballgame. Married? How are your parents? And the inevitable. She didn't want to but she didn't think she could handle it. Wasn't much help where I was. Yeah, drugs. Mostly an income property by the park now, high school English with DPS then. Written you lots of notes, a few stories. Had plenty of things to say. Always wondered where you were, how you were doing, if you could ever forgive me.

At intermission, Frances tells me about the travesty of the National Spelling Bee.

"It's racist crap," Frances says. "The Jamaican girl wins and they disqualify her. If that was a white boy from the burbs no way would he have been disqualified. It's bullshit."

I ask what the problem was and, shaking her head, Frances says, "It had to do with the cutoff dates, not even how to spell a word. It's lame," she says, "lame-ass racist bullshit. Same as it ever was."

"What was her word, the winning word?"

"Chiaro something."

"Chiaroscuro?"

"Yeah, what is that?"

"Not sure exactly. Has to do with painting, shading I think. How are you doing with tomorrow?"

"I'd be alright with it if you'd quit bringing it up."

"This is the first time I've said anything."

"Yeah, well, the thought of a bunch of medical types staring down at my snatch, burning my cervix isn't exactly a turn on, you know."

After the play, when we're in bed, I get my old teaching copy of *The Tempest*, read the parts I missed or couldn't hear.

Frances says, "Why you reading that, you just saw the play?"

I find Prospero's speech at the end, read it a couple times, hear Shakespeare speaking, his voice. It sounds like a farewell speech. *As you from crimes would pardoned be,/Let your indulgence set me free.* I want to read it to Frances. "Listen," I say, but she's asleep. I put my hand on her face, stroke her hair. *As you from crimes would pardoned be,/Let your indulgence set me free.*

8.

It's Sunday evening and we sit on a blanket at City Park, listen to Hazel Miller and her band. We've brought a picnic basket, people dance all around us. The band covers a slow song, Gladys Knight, and Frances asks me to dance. Frances is telling me that her Pap test was not good, that the laser didn't get it all.

"What do the results mean?" I say.

"It probably means they'll have to do a hysterectomy, take out my uterus and cervix but leave my ovaries and fallopian tubes."

"When do they want to do it?"

"In a month. I'll be there for a couple days."

I can feel Frances struggling to separate from me and I hold her. I can see her examining my face, hairy ears and receding hairline. The music changes to a fast song; we continue to dance slow.

"I guess that's it for sure then isn't it?" Frances says, laughing and crying at the same time. "No birthin' babies, no queen bee, no Francie the nurturer, no making Dorothy happy."

I pat her, say "It's all right, Frances, it's all right."

"No family basketball team, no paper routes, no one to take over the estate. I'm sure R.O.'s gonna be upset."

We sit back down on the blanket, in the dark, under the cool stars. I stretch out, Frances lies on top of me. We doze briefly, stir when people begin to leave. After waking we gather our things, walk to the car holding hands, drive home in silence. Frances wants to stay with me, sleep with me, but doesn't want to cuddle. I read late under the lamp, fall asleep with a book in my hands. When I wake, Frances is talking in her sleep and stops when I touch her.

I fall back to sleep and in the night dream of something inside her that resembles spoiled meat. In the morning I tell Frances about the dark spot.

"Do you think you were inside my uterus?" Frances says.

"I don't know," I say, "it did seem cave-like."

"Why didn't you keep going, check out my intestines and my heart, see what was in my head?"

"My flashlight batteries were running down. Besides, I could see a sign up ahead that said, 'Turn back now.'"

Frances puts the pillow over my face and playfully tries to smother me. When she lets me up I say, "No, I think it actually said 'Turn back now, whitey.'"

Frances wraps her arms and legs tightly around me and tells me that aside from the laser procedure, she's never had any kind of major surgery, never even had a broken bone.

"I'm afraid, Low, afraid I won't wake up or they won't get it all and I'll die like my mother did."

"Something tells me you'll be all right, you'll come out of it."

"I hope you're right. You'll be there during the operation?"

"I'll be there the whole time, Frances. I'll see you on the other side."

"Yeah," Frances says, "that's what I'm afraid of. Which other side?"

9.

It's Thursday and my mother has stopped by for lunch. She has made a cobbler from last year's rhubarb, begins straightening things, picking up, as I talk on the phone. One of the pipes in an apartment leaked and ruined the sheetrock in the unit below it. I'm arranging to have it repaired. When I get off the phone, she asks how it went with Gail.

"It was fine," I say, "we had a couple drinks, talked. It was a good chance to get to know her. Mom, did you ever see a black Lab around here last year?"

"No," Dorothy says, "and she told me the same story. My guess is that the likely suspects in the disappearing tomatoes case are Ervin and maybe the dog as a long shot. Number one suspect being Ervin. Gail's got a little crush on you, Low. I think she's thinking of asking you over for dinner."

"I hope you didn't say anything, I hope you didn't give her the wrong idea."

"I didn't say anything, just that I thought you had a good time."

"And?"

"And what?"

"What else did you say?"

"I just said you'd probably enjoy that, that'd be something you'd like."

"This is great cobbler, Mom. I love it when you make this cobbler."

"I just think you and Gail—"

"Mom, I have a good relationship with Frances. I'm not looking for another relationship. What is it with you? Is it because she's black, or that she's too old and can't have kids, or both?"

"I don't mind that Frances is black, I just want you to find somebody you can begin again with, somebody you can be with for a long time, you're still young enough."

"What makes you think Frances and I won't be together for a long time?"

"I'm not saying anything about Frances, Lowell, that's not it. I love Francie."

"But what? You'd like me to be with someone younger, who can still have babies, right? Because neither Deanne nor I have any kids and you'd like to have some grandkids, right?"

"Let's just finish our lunch. Let's not talk about this and ruin our lunch."

Dorothy tells me that she and some of her friends went to the Gustav Klimt exhibit at the art museum and loved it.

"He was a German fellow that had a thing with kissing," Dorothy says, "kissing and quilts."

"I think he was Austrian, Mom, and I'm not sure what you mean about quilts."

"His paintings, they all have these really pretty quilts wrapped around the people and on the floors and walls."

"Yeah, they did sort of look like quilts, as I recall."

"Where did you see him?"

"Remember that summer I went to Europe?"

"How could I forget. After that was when you started to have your trouble."

"After I came back from Amsterdam, when I was walking around Munich, I went to the art museum and they had a few of his paintings there. Was the picture of the woman with the big hat at this show?"

"Which one? The one with the black feather boa or the tall one?"

"The tall one."

"No, only the one with the feather boa."

"I thought that was one of the best pieces in the museum, and they had Rembrandts and Monets."

While I'm talking to my mother I think about a courtyard in Munich not far from the art museum. I'm still a young man and the wind ruffles my hair, buffets my ears. I've been up all night smoking opium with newfound friends, having a good time. That afternoon I'd gone into the museum to wander around. As I stand leaning against the wall I tell myself I still have time, there's plenty of time, I can stop whenever I want.

I ask my mother if she wants to hear about a crazy little encounter I had after coming out of the museum. I've never told anyone about the incident and sometimes I'm not sure it happened.

"Yes," she says, "as long as it's not about drugs. And then I'm going to tell a joke."

"It's not about drugs, Mom. I'd just finished lunch in this beer hall and was walking down a street near the center of Munich. It was early February and snowing. I stepped into a courtyard to get out of the wind and the cold, I was looking for an address. Around me there were apartments on three floors built out of a light-colored stone. They weren't new apartments but they didn't seem like they were centuries old either. Each had a big window that looked down on the courtyard and all of them except one had blinds or shutters. The second floor apartment that was the exception had maroon velvet curtains and while I was standing there a woman drew them open and she was naked. It was like a scene from one of the paintings in the museum."

"Completely naked?"

"Yes, completely naked. She was very white and had a hairbrush in one hand. I think she'd just gotten out of the bath. We both stood there, her looking down at me, me looking up at her."

"How long?"

"I don't know, maybe a minute. It was the most amazing thing. I wanted to reach up to her, be with her. And her eyes and face said the same thing back to me. Then something, a gust of wind, a pigeon, broke the moment and she stepped away from the window."

"Was she a young woman or older?"

"She was younger, maybe about the same age as me."

"And that was it, she didn't come back and you didn't knock on her door or anything?"

"I started to leave, I was on my way out of the courtyard and she came to the window in a bathrobe and pulled the drapes closed. But we had another moment before she got them closed all the way. It was like a magnet."

"Do you think it was sexual, the whole thing, or something else?"

"Sexual and something else. Why?"

"Has that ever happened again, that kind of connection?"

"Never, not like that."

"That was probably a once in a lifetime thing. You're lucky you didn't miss it, people often do."

"Did that ever happen to you?" I say to my mother.

She looks away and says, "No."

"Not with Dad?"

There is a long pause before she says faintly, "No."

"And now that joke," Dorothy says. "One of the gals we went to the art museum with, Clorys, told this one at lunch. An old man goes to the doctor for a physical. The doctor says, 'You look great for a man of seventy-five.' No, wait. I always screw these jokes up. The doctor says, 'You look great for a man of sixty.' The old man tells the doctor he's seventy-five. The doctor says, 'Seventy-five, that means your father probably lived to be a ripe old age.' The old man says, 'Who says he's dead?' The doctor says, 'Your father's not dead? How old is he?' The old man tells him he's a hundred. 'Your father's a hundred?' the doctor says."

Dorothy is telling the joke, trying hard not to cry.

"'That probably means your grandfather was pretty old when he died.' The old man says, 'Who says he's dead?' The doctor says, 'Your grandfather's not dead?' 'Nope,' the old man says, 'he's one hundred and twenty-five years old and would like to get married.' No, damn it, I screwed it up again. 'He's one hundred and twenty-five years old and is getting married next week.' 'Getting married?' the doctor says. 'Why would a man that old want to get married?' The old man says, 'Who says he wants to.'"

Dorothy holds her hands in front of her face, weeps softly. I put my hand on her shoulder, rub her back. I would like to comfort her but am not sure what to say, and then we look at each other and laugh. My father was not terribly emotional or romantic and I remember the night my mother had packed a bag and was prepared to leave until Deanne and I talked her out of it.

"Your father was a wonderful man," Dorothy says, "a wonderful man."

•————•

There is another note from my tenant under the door:

    Lo, I was hopg maybe next mo we could do a little tradng. I know
    I got behind last time and it took me awhile. If your up for it I think I

could pick up a satlite dish or poss do some work on that fence, which is gettg weathred as you know. I could work on the fence in the eves and take it out of the rent or install the dish if my buddy turns lose of it, whichever is your pref.

If we don't work that out I was wonderg if the cable can be part of the rent anyway if we don't get the dish. The people upstairs seems to have theirs on 24hrsaday, and some foreign. I asked if I could look at hers for a minute, but because she is something else I think she didnot undrstnd and got pissed. French maybe, but I'm not sure abt her husband anymore. I hve seen some of his friends and wonder.

That cage of birds you saw is my new fiance Angela's. She is thinkg to raise a few as a trial, now tht she is not workg and has the time while she is with me temp. Maybe pick up some spare bucks. Im assumg there is no pet dep. And the best part is we wont need no scoop for the yard (joke).

Anyhoo, hve a good one and say thanks to your mother for that info. Ervin.

P.S Abt your questn. I only ate a couple tomatos, mostly the overipe ones, or that were on the ground. A few of the others.

10.

"It didn't end well," I say to my mother. "In fact we didn't get through dinner at all."

I've taken my mother to the health food market, we're in the produce section, and Dorothy has asked how Gail's special dinner went, she practically insisted I come. Dorothy wants to make a big salad with lunch. She picks out a nice shitake mushroom, a golden bell pepper, and elephant garlic for the pasta. The arugula looks pitted and she's disappointed. She finds a fresh baguette, pesto.

"You didn't get through dinner?"

"No, we didn't get to that," I say. "She'd been drinking wine before I got there and was upset when I said I was leaving and wasn't going to sleep with her."

As we push the cart and shop I can see Gail sitting on the sofa in her apartment, talking, eating crackers and dip, drinking wine. She asks me to spend the night, make love to her. When she puts her arms around me I ask her not to, then say I'm leaving when she doesn't. She tries to stop me, stands in front of the door. It's a difficult moment.

"I'm worried about her," Dorothy says. "I think she's been sleeping a lot during the day and missing work. She hasn't washed her hair for weeks."

"Maybe you could knock on her door, check on her, just to make sure she's all right."

"I was thinking you should do that."

"Right now I'm a little hesitant. I have her brother's number if you want to get in touch with her family."

"Well, I'll call her brother if she doesn't look any better by the end of the week, but as the landlord it seems like you have some responsibility."

At home Dorothy prepares the pasta, tells me what she wants in the salad. The next day is the anniversary of my father's death. Dorothy muses about Paul, what a funny man he was.

"He would stay up very late during the summer," Dorothy says, "do you remember that?"

"Yeah, and wander around in his shorts drinking root beer all night doing puzzles in those little books."

"He loved root beer and little cans of pork and beans. He would heat them right on the burner."

"Why did he do that, what was that about?"

"I think it was an Army thing. When I'd check on him I'd find him sitting on a folding chair in the garage, looking at pictures and going through his box from the war, eating the beans with a spoon from the can. When I checked on him one night and he didn't recognize me, that was when I first knew something was wrong."

"When was that?"

"Eight years ago. He was alright most of the time at first and I tried to say it was because he was staying up so late, but then he began sleeping on a recliner in the garage. He thought I was a woman from the neighborhood."

"He started calling Deanne and me by his sisters' and brothers' names," I say, "that was the first real clue we had. I think you did a pretty good job of hiding it."

"I was afraid. Afraid if I said something he truly would be sick and I wasn't ready for that. I still wanted him to be my husband and I didn't know what I'd do without him."

"If you had to do it all over again, Mom, knowing what you know, would you live your life the same, marry the same?"

"Exactly the same."

"No regrets?"

"Frank Sinatra was a fool. I've had more than a few regrets, but I'd do it exactly the same. I'd marry your father all over again."

There is a message on my phone, in two installments:

#1: Sorry, Low, I'm sorry. I know I shouldn't have said those things and done those things. I just... More than anything I just needed someone to hold me. I know you have a girlfriend and everything. I haven't been sleeping all that good at night and I thought, I know this is crazy, I just thought if you would lie next to me and hold me till I went to sleep. I didn't really care about the other things but I know how it came across. I drank wine without eating and I shouldn't have done that. Now you probably think I just made dinner to get you to have sex with me or something and I apologize, I apologize.

#2: I also wanted to say when I used to live above the Day-Old store, I would sit in my window and the giant neon for Wonder-Hostess was right above me on the roof. Red and blue. At night the sign lit up my apartment and turned me this funny color. My skin and lips and hands. With the buzz from the neon, it made me think this is how it feels to be going crazy. I would put soft wax in my ears so I could sleep, but I could hear the noise anyway, or thought I could. I've heard that buzzing again the last few nights and don't know if it's the fridge or me or what. Maybe you could check it.

Please don't think I'm crazy for saying what I said and did. I love your mother and I love my apartment. I promise not to do or say anything like that again. Sorry Low. Sorry.

11.

In the hospital I'm waiting in Frances's room when they bring her back from surgery. The cancer had metastasized, spread from the lining of the cervix into deeper connective tissue. There is a small stitched incision on her stomach. Attendants lift her from the gurney onto the bed. Frances is awake, the anesthesia has almost worn off. She smiles at me and I hold her hand.

"Don't try anything," Frances says.

"I'm going to wait till you fall asleep," I say.

"Figures."

I draw the curtain around Frances, climb up on the bed next to her. Frances leans against me, I put my arm around her.

"You're a nice boy," Frances says.

"That's what you say now."

The post-op nurse enters the room, pulls the drape back, asks me to get off the bed.

"He's fine just where he is," Frances says.

"Your friend will have to come off the bed in order for you to rest," the nurse says. "You've just been through major surgery."

"Nurse," Frances says, "don't make me get up out of here."

The nurse leaves and returns with the ward's head nurse. I've moved to a chair next to the bed.

"I'll have to ask you to leave," the head nurse says, "if you can't abide by hospital policy."

"He leaves, I leave," Frances says.

When the nurses leave the room I say, "That would've been interesting if you'd followed through on your threat. An escaped hysterectomy patient on the streets of Denver. Police would have been on the lookout for a woman flashing a stomach incision."

"Lowell," Frances says, "don't make me laugh. It says on the sheet no sex and no laughing for six weeks. I'll have to ask you to leave if you can't abide by hospital policy."

A young woman enters the room, explains she's going to give Frances a light sponge bath and would I mind waiting in the visitors' room.

"Let him do it," Frances says.

"Oh, I couldn't do that," the young woman says.

"Why not?" Frances says. "And don't say hospital policy."

"He might injure you," she says. "There are specific procedures for a post-op bath. And in this hospital, men do not bathe women."

"Well," Frances says, "they don't know what they're missing."

"Tell you what I'll do," I say. "I'll buy your lunch if you take your break right now and leave your equipment. When you come back, miraculously, Ms. Harris will have been bathed."

"I could get in a lot of trouble," the young woman says.

"You know how hard it's going to be to give me a bath if I don't want a bath?" Frances says.

I put ten dollars in the woman's smock and take her sponge and bucket.

I pull the bedding back, maneuver the rubber sheet under Frances. She turns slightly on her side, I untie her gown. With the soft sponge and warm water, I begin with her feet. Frances has slender brown feet with toenails painted a flecked blue. I notice the squiggle in the vein that crosses one ankle, the crimped shape of both second toes, the flatness of her arches. I hold the heel of a foot with one hand, lightly sponge the top and sole. Frances shudders when I touch the bottom of her feet. Her eyes are closed, hands folded on her chest.

I wash her ankles, calves, thighs, and her dark crotch. I lift Frances's leg to get the back side and notice a reddish discharge between her legs, dab the liquid up.

I would like to touch the incision, wash the stitches, but only wash around them. Frances half-turns and I bathe her cheeks, back, neck, and shoulders. When she turns again I squeeze water onto her breasts, wipe them down. After I've dried Frances, I help her back into her gown. She's very tired and before the young woman returns has fallen into a deep sleep. I finish reading the paper, kiss her, and leave.

12.

When I return from taking Frances home there's mail in the box and messages on the phone. The first message is from someone who has the wrong number and has left a lengthy, drunken speech about directions to a party.

The second is from Linnie. Linnie says "Hello, hope you're well." She inquires about my mother and offers her condolences for Marty.

And then: "Low—Davis made contact today. An agency that finds birth parents called and asked if it was all right if they put him in touch with me. I said yes and he called this morning. We talked and we're going to have him over. He asked if I knew where you were, if we were still in touch, and I said yes. I gave him your number, I hope that's all right."

I open the blinds in the living room, stand in the slatted light. I put a piano piece with big chords on the stereo and pause a moment, think of going by the Eighth for company, then think better of it.

Somewhere in the vicinity of my heart there's a softening and I'd like to put my arms around Linnie, apologize for everything. When Davis and I talk it won't be about erasing the past, but maybe there could be a small window, a point of contact, a place for us to begin again. Something I'd like.

I sort through the letters, toss the ads and envelopes addressed to Resident. I'm surprised to see an envelope from a small magazine I submitted a story to. One of my pieces about the Eighth has been accepted.

There's a note from my mother on the table. Someone found her cat, placed an ad in the paper after these many weeks. She also adds the new tenant in Gail's apartment got moved in okay.

I can tell by the handwriting on the envelope there's a letter from Gail. She says she's feeling better, still staying with her brother. Will probably start back to work in a couple weeks, though at a different job. She thanks me three times for my letter and the check for the security deposit, apologizes twice for any problems she might have caused. She would like to stop by and visit, if that's all right. Closes with "Bye for now." And there's a P.S.: "If you ever want to talk about the 'it's a long story,' give a call."

Confluence

By Mark Hummel

He had come looking for something he could not name. Now some might say that meant he was searching for nothing at all, that looking was an excuse for a man who was a vagrant in their eyes, the kind of man they might nod at on the street but not offer a smile, a man from whom they averted their eyes. This was the town he identified with childhood, having been gone so long and having lived so many places most now blended one into another like a water color caught in the rain. He paced its streets trying to find those features that prodded vague memories and feelings of familiarity. He could not name his age when he lived there last, though he guessed he had been about seven. His mother was alive then, that much he remembered clearly, though he struggled to recall her face. They had moved that first time after her death, then kept on moving, like songbirds, his old man used to say, songbirds following the sun and food. And he'd kept on moving with his own two boys. Moving was all they'd known. If you asked him his age, he might have given you a number and it might prove a number somewhere near his true age, which was forty-two, though it would be but an honest guess on his part. When he and the boys first arrived in town some two months prior, he'd tried to do the math. He kicked along gravel alleys in the older residential sections of town trying to remember his sums from those few portions of years his father had kept him in school, trying both to remember simple math and images of places long removed. At length he had given up, satisfied only that he had lived there somewhere prior to the war, perhaps 1914 or 1915, making him nearly the same age then as his youngest boy now.

The man spent most of his time walking, most often in a neighborhood blocks removed from the small grid of streets that formed the downtown. The neighborhood stumbled down a hillside toward the river and its thickets of willows and cottonwoods. Narrow streets kept in strict grids, but grids that did not match the surrounding streets such that each jogged a half block as it descended the hill, as if the entire development while still on paper in neatly drawn lines had been caught in a bad fold, like a map that could not retain its creases. Each house inhabited a skinny but deep lot, the front porches set close to the street. There were no sidewalks and only about half the streets were paved. Every house had a ramshackle garage opening onto a rutted alley, and there were pieced-together sheds or lean-tos and most often chickens in the backyards, evidence of country folk become city folk, short enough removed to retain the chickens, but long enough removed to get them out of the front yard.

Every time he entered this neighborhood a physical sensation crept through his body. He had, he thought, narrowed his choices to three or four possibilities. So many years. So much moving, so much living in backrooms and rail cars and barns and, in the best of times, bunkhouses with other workers where there were women present to mind the boys. He couldn't be sure. Each of the houses had covered front porches shaded by trees, which were just now dropping color-turned leaves. Most of the harvest had been in for two weeks. The house he stood before, like the rest, had the quality of mild neglect about it. Suckers sprouted in thickets from the tree roots and the lawn was sparse, an echo of what little fading paint the house bore. Had this been the tree where he and his siblings roped together a house? Could this be the porch where his father smoked in the evenings and his folks played bridge with the neighbors on Saturdays?

He'd become a ghost haunting those streets. He knew better. In his tattered and oft-mended clothes, the one work boot, the right one, tied together with a length of rope, he made people nervous. It wouldn't be long before the women would call the law or some of the men would put a beating on him. He knew no good would come of him walking these streets but still he found his feet carrying him there each morning.

•———•

Rather than call the law, whom she distrusted, associating, in her mind, all who wore uniforms with the army, which had taken her only son from her, Edith White-head called her neighbor.

"Tom," she hollered. It was Thursday evening and she was taking the laundry off the line when she saw him moving beyond the fence that divided their yards. "Tom, there's been a man coming round here every morning that ain't up to no good."

Tom leaned the hand rake he wielded against a stump and approached the fence. He was a tall man and his head and shoulders showed above the top plank, and he curled one hand over its edge. Edith alternated between trying to hold a conversation between the plank boards and stepping back far enough toward a lilac where she could, by tilting her head enough, look him in the face.

"I'm telling you, he's trouble. He slinks around here every morning about nine o'clock. I seen him there through the kitchen window every day this week. Why just yesterday I was fixing brine water for my pickles—them sweet ones you like so well—and there he sits on the curb across the street from your place. I think maybe he's looking at me. Gives me the jeepers."

"No law against sitting, Edith. You know Waters has somebody working at his place, reroofing that leaky bedroom he added. Waters's too feeble to get up there himself. Maybe it's his man."

"Naw. This ain't no hired man."

"What's this feller look like? Maybe I've seen him around."

"Skinny feller. Skinny as a garden snake. Dirty. Crooked nose like he done had it broke for him more than once. I tell you he's scheming."

"I'm sure there's nothing to worry about."

"Nothing to worry about? You won't be saying that when I turn up dead and my house robbed."

"Well, why don't you call the police then? He comes around here tomorrow and you just pick up the phone."

"The police. Law don't come down round here unless somebody already dead."

"You call. They'll send somebody."

"Not unless one of them's going fishing or thinking about taking a nap down by the river. They don't come see about us and our problems." Edith puckered her face and wiped both her hands down the length of her apron.

Tom looked past her, out across her yard and toward the foothills where the sun was beginning to fade and cast the world in limbs of dust-laden soft light. In this light, each rise and depression of the foothills stood out in a different dark shade, row after row of ridge and canyon rising ever upward toward the high peaks beyond, which stood sharp in outline against the evening sky. He was aware of the cool of the coming night. There had been an early freeze and then this lovely Indian summer.

He lowered his gaze back to Edith once more. "I'm sure there is nothing to worry about."

"Nothing to worry about? You just watch this here laundry line, Tom Matthews. One night this here laundry will still be on the line when you go to bed. Be there next morning too. And by the time you finally decide to come check on this old lady, there'll be flies feasting on me. How you gonna feel then, Tom?"

"Well," Tom let out an audible sigh. "What do you want me to do about him? Shoot him for having bad teeth and a bent nose?"

This sent Edith into another tirade, this time leading to a general commentary about the state of the world and people getting killed in their own beds. Finally she closed by saying, "If you were to come round tomorrow, big feller like you, you'd scare him off."

"You know I've got to work."

"Hell, Tom. You own the shop. You come and go as you please."

Tom could tell that Edith was prepared to stand there, her thin neck craned like a bird all night. "I'll try to get away."

"You come by about nine, Tom. Man's as regular as clockwork."

———•———

The boys, so dirty their skin reflected the color of the dirt in which they were building some sort of a city, played mere feet from the river in a thick copse of trees. A piece of heavy machinery, probably a loader or a dump truck hauling rock out of the river bottom, had passed through this low river country in recent days, and the boys collected the compacted earth left by the heavy tire grooves and stacked them forming buildings and walls, some topped with empty match boxes and food tins. The younger boy was digging deep trenches around their creation, scooping at the dark heavy soil with a coffee can. Now and again he'd leave with the can and then return with it dripping river water that he poured into his reservoirs. His brother was scraping absently at a stick with a rusted pocket knife. As the younger boy poured another can of water, black mud splashing onto the cuffs of his pants, his brother looked up from the wood and shouted, "Whatcha doin? You'll ruin it, moron. This ain't no castle. It's an army compound."

The smaller boy ignored him and began digging anew.

"We been workin on it for two days and you are ruinin it." Then, as if to punctuate his point, he stood up and stepped deliberately onto one of their clay buildings, flattening it. As if the destruction triggered an idea, he kicked at one of the dikes his brother had created, rupturing it. He smiled as the water swirled through the gap and filled the grid between their constructions. "Flood, flood, "he shouted. "Look out below. You'd better run." He walked alongside the advancing water as if encouraging it.

The smaller boy looked at his brother incredulously for a moment, then kicked at the levee of another lake and smiled as muddy water trickled into their town. As their little town flooded, they set about floating bits of grass and tree bark through its streets.

They had, inadvertently, created a landscape in miniature that mimicked their camp. Their meager possessions were strewn about the little grove, as if by spreading them out, there would seem more—a Dutch oven balanced on a downed tree, a couple of coffee tins, one filled with some mismatched pieces of silverware, a makeshift tent cut from a tarpaulin tied between two trees. Items placed as sporadically along the river as their play town now appeared.

A little later, the boy was carrying handfuls of ashes from the fire pit and was sprinkling them in the road beds where their flood had receded. His brother had again picked up his knife and stick.

"I'm hungry," the younger boy said.

"There's probably a couple a taters left in that fire if you dig in there."

"I'm sick of taters."

"Better be glad you got them."

"I hate them. That's all we done had forever."

"Eat grass then."

"But I'm hungry."

"Shut up already. He ain't bringin in no food."

"But he's workin right? Been workin steady."

"You some kind of dumb," the older boy said. He was a big boy, thick through the shoulders and arms though still young and still short. Big enough he'd already worked through most of the summer and parts of the fall with his father, at least in places that would hire a child. "He ain't worked in a week. Sugar beets is all in. Ain't no more work. Sides," he said, "you seen what he done with the money he had last week." He prodded at some empty bottles tossed into a clump of grass with his stick.

"I don't like it here."

"It's better down here by the river than up there on them windy bluffs where we was."

"I mean this town. I like the river plenty. I don't like this town."

"Not much different than most we been in, if you ask me. Papa talked about stayin on and gettin us back into school. Doubt it will happen. I reckon we'll be headed south soon."

"It's cold here," his younger brother whined. "I 'bout froze last night. When I got up, he was already gone and the fire was dead. Where's he goin if he's not workin?"

"Probably drinkin."

"Why can't he buy some food? We was eatin good there for awhile. What about you? Didn't they pay you your money?"

"Papa took that too."

"Well, I'm gonna get me somethin to eat," the youngest boy said.

"Oh. Just how you fixin on doin that?"

"I seen that place on the other side of the river, there across that road, that busy road we walked in on with Papa when we come down here. All them big trucks haulin food and hay. You seen it. They got carrots stacked in piles as high as a tree there. Onions too. And I seen 'em haulin beans into them tall buildings. I'm gonna get me some that food."

"How you do that?"

"I'll just sneak over there and take some. They got so much they never miss it."

"You know Papa said we supposed to stay here. Said not to cross the river," his brother said. "He'll tan your hide, he catch you."

"It's gonna be some good eatin. You comin?"

"You're a chicken. You'll never go."

"Wanna bet?"

"Ain't got nothin to bet."

"How bout that knife?" the little boy said.

"This here my knife. I done found it."

"Well, I'm goin anyhow."

"Good luck," his brother replied. He spat on the ground and watched as his little brother retreated through the trees and then angled through the tall, brown grass toward the river. He could see the blue of his shirt in glimpses through the trees for a long while advancing west along the river bottom. "He'll never get across that river," he said aloud, spit again, then placed a long stem of grass between his teeth and took back up his stick.

———•———

The man sat at the curb directly across from Tom's front door, staring off into the distance, like he could see right though the house. Tom, approaching in his pickup, found himself following the man's stare despite himself, as if the man could look straight down that shotgun hall through the front door and out the back to where he had an Esso sign hanging on the garage. But of course the door was closed. Had been closed most of the fifteen years he'd owned the house. His few friends came and went by the back door and alley and, even in the years when his wife and son lived with him, back before she'd gone home to New Mexico to her family, they rarely used the front door.

The house was neat but plain. He kept the foundation plantings trimmed and the grass mowed. Not a lot of color but green he noted now, looking at the house as if seeing it anew. The house was a simple square and seemed to squat on the lot. It was, he noted, as he did each time he drove the street and every time he mowed, badly in need of paint, the green trim mostly absent and the white clapboard faded to a dull gray, weathered and peeling.

The man sat the curb and did not change the direction of his focus when Tom pulled even with him. Tom had his hand dangling out the window trailing a cigarette.

The man wore coveralls that had been patched heavily in the knees, a plaid shirt of uncertain color and one skinned but still sound leather work boot. His hair was kept short but chopped unevenly like it had been shorn with a buck knife. He had an angular face that would look better if there were more flesh on it. Tom had seen him about the streets in recent weeks near downtown and the cabinet shop he owned. He'd seen him but didn't recognize him as a local, though few of the farmers about town dressed much better or much differently. "Howdy," he tried. "Help you find something?"

The man started, as if asleep. "No, sir." He retrieved a blue handkerchief from a back pocket and wiped his nose.

"You lost?"

"No, sir. Just restin."

"Seen you been doing a lot of that."

"Might be. Who's askin?"

"Oh, just nobody. Folks who live around here are wondering what you were doing."

"Not doin anything."

"I can see that."

The men were silent for awhile. Tom smoked. The man returned the handkerchief to his pocket.

"Don't suppose I could get a smoke off you," the man asked, standing.

Tom shook him one out of the pack he kept in the visor, handed him his own for a light.

"Ummm," the man sighed. "That sure tastes good. I thank you."

Tom watched him enjoy the cigarette, sizing him up. "You new around here?"

"Well," the man said, "that depends. I been up here workin the harvest since August. That's not quite right. I done worked the cherries earlier, then went east over toward Greeley and Fort Morgan. But I was born here and lived here some when I was little." He took another drag on the cigarette. "I been thinkin maybe I used to live in this here house. Can't be sure."

"That right?"

"Place needs paint. I seem to remember yellow or somethin toward yellow anyhow. Memory's not so good. Like I said, I can't be sure."

"I've been meaning to paint."

"This your place?"

"Yeah."

"You buy it from a man named Jones?"

"No. Bought it from a family by the name of Felder. They hadn't been in it for very long. The place had changed hands a couple of time before that as I recall, bought and sold more than once during the Depression."

The pickup sat idling, its engine running smooth and not loud. A faint breeze came in from the west and the morning remained cool but fair. An occasional leaf swirled down out of the overhanging trees. One landed on the pickup hood and Tom noted it.

"It's the damndest thing," the man said. "How you can't remember. Like sometimes I walk down this street and it feels like some place I've been before. I try to recall that feelin. You know, how you felt when you saw a place or you done somethin for the very first time. But you can't. Like I can't picture any of these other houses but that corner up there looks right, that hedge and all and the red bricks set there against the street, but I can't get a hold of anythin else. And I think I remember yellow on your house there but I can't know. Yet sometimes, like the other day I walked past the smell of somethin cookin outside somebody's window and all the sudden I remembered every detail of our old kitchen and I could even hear my mama's voice again callin me to supper." He looked at Tom. "Funny, ain't it?"

Tom extinguished his cigarette against the back of the mirror and flicked the butt into the truck bed. "Cool weather like this here would be the time to paint."

"Reckon it would," the man agreed.

"You paint any?"

"Some. A good deal of barns and outbuildings."

"I suppose one wall is pretty much the same as another."

"I reckon."

"It would take a lot of scraping and cleaning. That's going to add some time. You be here before seven tomorrow?"

"Yes, sir. That's no problem. I'm a hard worker, sir."

"You drink?"

"Not when I'm workin."

"Well, you be here. I'll figure a fair wage for the whole job. Pay you cash when it's done. If that price seems fair to you in the morning, you can start right in. I expect a job done right."

"Yes, sir," he said and shook Tom's hand. The pickup pulled away, Tom's arm still hanging out the open window. He raised it in a stiff wave without looking.

•————•

At noon the next day he stopped back by his house to check on the man's progress and to drop off the paint he bought at the hardware store that morning. Small drifts of peeled and dried paint blanketed the foundation wall. The south side and the front were done and the man was at work on the north side employing a scraper with fervor. Edith was waiting for Tom by the time he got the tailgate open.

"Tom Matthews. You think this is a hoot, don't you. Scaring an old woman this way. It wasn't enough to have a murdering thief in the neighborhood plotting how he was going to rob me. No, you gotta bring him right up in the front yard for a better look."

"Edith," Tom said, hefting the cans of paint, "he's just a fellow down on his luck."

"Drunkard more like it."

"May be. But looks to me he's doing a good job. You know you've been nagging at me to paint for years. You ought to be happy."

"Happy? Happy—"

Tom shrugged past her with the paint and left her at the curb. The man was on a ladder scraping just below the soffit.

"Looking good, bub," Tom said. "You're making good progress."

"I expect you're gonna want to replace some wood there and again. Some bad spots where the weather been on it. You might want to have a look at the window sashes on the west side too."

"I expect you're right. Might as well do it proper." Tom made two more trips from the truck and reconnoitered the supplies. "You need anything?"

"No, sir."

"How late you figuring on working?"

"I can work as late as you want."

"Well, I'm paying you for the job, not by the hour, so you don't have to work late. I thought I might come get my hands in on it too when I get off. Get started on the trim at least. I'll mill some trim for those spots of rot at the shop."

"I'll be here."

"You got water? You find the spigot?"

"Yes, sir." The man stepped off the ladder. There were paint flecks graying his hair. "I was wonderin if I might bring my boys with me tomorrow. The older one can help and the younger one ain't no trouble. They mind me well."

"Sure," he said. "Bring them with you. But mind the neighbor," he added. "She don't take well to strangers."

———•———

Afternoon and the boy was hungry. The feeling was familiar, too familiar, and often he would drink water to have something in his stomach and always hunger made him mean and short fused. They'd had a thin broth the night before, a few sparse vegetables once and again in spoonfuls but mainly water. No breakfast except coffee. Sometimes when he was hungry he'd imagine chewing gum. He could taste the spicy sweet juices in his throat when he tried hard enough. Once that summer when the cherries were coming in he'd been allowed to work too, carrying the empty bushel baskets back out to the men and hauling them water. There was a foreman who was always giving him sticks of gum. It didn't help when he was hungry but tasted so good he'd forget for a time.

Yesterday he had never found a place to cross the river, except on the railway bridge, but there were men who lived down there and they scared him. The river was not deep or fast this time of year. Sand bars showed here and there across its width and the water meandered between them. But he still couldn't find a place to cross where he wouldn't get wet, and even the water at this speed worried him. He'd seen where the river had carried whole trees and pushed piles of driftwood together like bleached bones.

So today he hiked down river though the thickets of willows and sumac and cottonwood until he found a bridge. He worked his way up the far bank trying to stay off the busy road that paralleled the river and trying to see also if he could pick out their little camp on the opposite shore, line himself up with the smokestacks of the sugar plant as a landmark. He couldn't recall how far up the road he had seen the silos and the buildings where he knew he would find food. Wouldn't his brother be jealous if he came back with a full belly and some more in his pockets? Twice he crossed weed-twined barbed wire fences that were nearly invisible in the thickets of growth. He'd cut his ankle on one strand, and after the fifth time of having to negotiate cattail-laden backwaters and dense stands of scrub trees, he finally decided to take to the road edge where the walking was easier. He played games of hide and seek, ducking into the dried grass stalks off the steep road bed when he heard the sound of an engine approaching. A lot of walking. Yet he never did find the food he was looking for.

— • —

On Saturday they continued to paint. Tom closed the shop at noon as he did every Saturday, paid his two carpenters for the week, and planned on helping paint until four or five. The man had proved steady but slow, slower as the week wore on. The older boy was a capable worker as long as they kept him away from any edges where paint colors met. He was a big boy, broad shouldered and quiet. Tom guessed him to be twelve or thirteen, about the age of his own son.

How many years had it been now? Eight. He sent money to his son's grandmother every month and she wrote once or twice a year, letters that were polite, but that didn't say much. He appreciated the pictures she sent. He wrote the boy every birthday and Christmas and sent presents, but the boy never replied. He wondered if his son was quiet like this boy. He watched him work from across the yard. There was a small garden plot and a clothesline. He'd always intended to build a swing set and a sand box but hadn't gotten to it, and then his son was gone, though, he supposed, he had been getting to an age where he might not have been interested anyway.

The boy's little brother talked incessantly, most often to himself. The brothers looked nothing alike. Different mothers, Tom concluded, for even their mannerisms were opposite. The boy seemed to talk to his father through his older brother most of the time. He looked to Tom like some sort of crazed bird, awkward and paranoid and constantly moving.

At one o'clock Tom served them a tray filled with cold cuts, bread, crackers, cheese, and apple slices. The little family ate ravenously, man and boy alike, and when there was but one apple left, the father took it from the youngest boy's hand and ate it in one bite. Tom had placed four beers and two sodas on ice. He'd seen the man's tongue flicker over his lips when he opened the little cooler, and he laughed at the boy's big eyes when he'd taken the first swig of the soda bottle. The beer was good and cold, ice water dripping from the bottle.

An hour later Tom reached into the cooler for another beer and it was empty. Then he saw the three empty bottles lined neatly on the sill near where the man was painting. It appeared he was repainting the same space over and over again.

The older boy rounded the corner of the house. He carried a brush and a half full paint bucket and there was a large streak of paint curling up his right cheek and onto his ear. "Go ahead and clean up these brushes," Tom said to the boy loud enough so the man could hear too. "We'll call it a day and start back in on Monday."

The man stood up from where he knelt against the back wall of the house and moved off toward the garage without a word. The little boy swung by his hands from a tree branch. As he swung, he sang continuously in a strange breaking falsetto, the words an incomprehensible child-gibberish.

———•———

On Monday morning, when he grew bored antagonizing his older brother and watching his father paint, he discovered the door was unlocked. He'd tried it three times already that morning. On the third try he'd opened it an inch or two, then pulled it closed again and walked away. On the fourth try, he put his head in the door. The door opened onto a long hall that extended all the way to the front door. There was a single wooden chair against the wall with two pairs of shoes next to it and a series of mounted coat hooks. He thought there were some kinds of pictures or paintings further down the hall, but the light was poor and he withdrew his head and pulled the door to again. He walked from the cement stoop back around the side of the house and took up his position at the kitchen window. On the counter between the stove and refrigerator there was a basket of apples and bananas. Next to it stood a loaf of bread with a piece of foil covering its cut end. He imagined the treasures that awaited him behind the closed cabinet doors and in the refrigerator.

On his fifth try he entered the hallway and closed the door behind him. His steps echoed on the wood floor. He tried to walk on his toes. The wood floor ended at the kitchen doorway, giving way to black and white checkered linoleum; yellow flecks dotted the black squares. His feet barely made a sound there. The kitchen smelled clean and aside from the bread and fruit, the counters were empty save for a tin of coffee and a block of knives.

He had just closed the door behind him again when he turned and saw his father at the base of the steps. Bread crumbs still clung to the boy's small mouth and he clutched an apple in his left hand with several uneven bites removed. The edge of a wax wrapper extended from the grimy pocket of his pants. His father stood with his arms at his side, hands curled into fists.

———•

Tom checked on the man's progress again on Monday mid-day. The house was essentially complete but for one open section in the middle of the rear wall where the older boy was at work. His father had started in on the garage. Tom nodded hello to the man and stopped next to the boy.

"Looks like you about got it licked."

"Yes, sir."

"You've done a good job."

"I'm tryin," the boy said. He looked nervous and avoided Tom's eyes as he spoke.

"Well," Tom said. "I brought the last of the new mill work and that section of soffit. You paint them for me and I'll put them up tonight."

"Yes, sir."

"Where's your little brother? He's not singing my ear off."

"He ain't comin."

"Not feeling well?"

"Naw. Them two," the boy indicated with a point of his chin toward his father, "got into it. He won't be comin round no more."

———•———

Tom left the neighborhood by way of Cherry Street, a dirt road closest to the river where the houses were further apart and there were still several vacant lots, each with a for sale sign that had been in place for twenty years, long since faded and overgrown. The town had continued to grow west toward the lake. He followed Cherry to Mill Road, which crossed the river and connected to the County Road. He had a special order of oak ready to pick up at McCollum's place for a job in the subdivision by the new country club. Most of the work was still in pine and birch, but more and more they were working in hardwoods for the bigger houses some folks were building.

He wondered where the man and his boys were staying. Each day when they left his place they headed south, toward the river, he suspected. He supposed they were squatting somewhere. He wondered where they could find a warm place for the winter, but then the man had talked about working the farms so he supposed that meant they went south for the winters. He wondered where: Texas? Arizona? Places he'd studied on a map a thousand times but had never been. He thought strongly about trying to get to New Mexico more than once. When he couldn't sleep he often tried to picture what it might look like. Folks he talked to said it was full of red rocks and mesas, but he had a time imagining it and could not form a picture he could place his son's face onto.

He caught sight of the boy just after he turned onto the county road. He looked to be limping. At the sight of the truck, the boy scampered off the road edge and down through the borrow pit to the trees beyond. Tom thought about rolling down the passenger window and hollering for him, but even in the brief glimpse as the boy fled, he saw the dark purple bruises that swelled the left side of his face, and he drove on.

———•———

Tom got out of his truck and lifted the door on the garage. The hinges needed oil and the door remained unpainted but for the trim around its two windows. The side of the garage facing away from his property remained unpainted as well, as was the shed. The weather was still good and there was still light in the evenings but even as Tom made a mental note to finish painting, he knew he would not. He'd paid the man the same night he'd seen the boy beside the road. Paid him cash and told him he'd done enough.

He found his oil can above the workbench and gave the hinges a generous squirt, wiping away the excess after he worked the door a few times. He retrieved a sack of beer from the pickup bed and could feel its cold through the paper. He'd seen the man twice that day, once sleeping on the bench next to the Ford dealership with a paper bag huddled in his crossed arms and just a few minutes ago stumbling down the sidewalk near the liquor store. "Damn," he said aloud as he closed the garage door.

He ate toast and two fried eggs for dinner that night, drank two of the beers, and fell asleep listening to the radio, an unread magazine slipping from his lap.

He was still asleep in the chair when the doorbell rang. He was momentarily disoriented at its sound, so it took some time to reach the front door and more time managing its lock and putting his shoulder into the wood to unstick it from the frame. "Just a minute," he mumbled, hearing a voice he did not recognize outside.

When he finally managed to open the door, a police officer greeted him by saying, "I'm sorry to bother you at this late hour, sir." He had his flashlight on—Tom had neglected to turn on the porch light—and the older boy stood timidly behind the policeman. "This young man claims to know you, sir. Made me bring him to this address, but he doesn't even know your name."

"I know him," Tom said. "What's he done?" Tom recognized the policeman but didn't know his name.

"Oh, he's fine. But his little brother has turned up missing."

"He took off," the boy interrupted. "I ain't seen him since."

"The boy claims they worked for you. That right?" asked the officer.

"Yeah. They did."

"You mind if I bother you a moment?" the policeman asked. "I need a minute alone if you don't mind."

Tom opened the door and let the man and the boy in the house. He turned on a lamp in the living room, turned off the static-ridden radio, and offered the boy a chair. He sat, stiffly. The men introduced themselves and the policeman, who identified himself as a captain, followed Tom to the kitchen where he slumped into a seat at the table.

"I'll make some coffee," Tom offered.

"That'd hit the spot."

Tom explained how he met the man and the work they'd done for him. He told him about the boy and seeing the bruises and about seeing the man on the street earlier.

"We've picked him up twice in the last week on vagrancy. Stopped him and warned him before that. Fact is, we picked him up tonight."

"I'm going to bring that boy something to eat," Tom said. He had cold chicken in the refrigerator. He poured a glass of milk. When he returned, he pulled a chair up to the table opposite the captain. "It will be a spell," he said, indicating the coffee.

The policeman smiled. "That boy came into the station tonight to report his brother missing. He looked scared. I suspect his dealings with the law haven't gone so well. I didn't have the heart to tell him we had his old man upstairs in the drunk tank," the captain said, lowering his voice.

The captain ran his hands back and forth across the surface of the table as if smoothing a sheet or a table cloth. It was a plain, white Formica table, big enough to seat four. "The thing is, we had a boy get run over earlier tonight over near Colorado Seed. Just at dark. Killed him. I suppose it's his boy. We had no idea he had family, most these drunks are on their own, but then that boy come in and described his brother, then described his father and we sort of put two and two together." The man sighed. The coffee began to gurgle in the percolator. "We tried to sober the old man up. Got him out of the cell and got some coffee in him. Spent two hours trying to get him coherent. I was fixing to get him in shape to go and identify the body. I went to see to this one," he said, hooking his thumb toward the living room, "and the old man took off. Disappeared like that," he said, snapping his fingers.

"I took that boy over round where he said they'd been camping by the river, then he insisted I bring him here. Said you'd help. Frankly, I was hoping you were family of some sort." He paused. "The thing is I need somebody who knows them. I need somebody to identify the boy's body."

The coffee pot was perking. They could smell the brewing liquid. A clock chimed elsewhere in the house. "I hate to trouble you. We'll find the father eventually. But these types, they can get away in a hurry when they want to. He'll turn up in another town near here more than likely. They'll bring him in on one thing or the other and know we're looking for him. Of course, I'm hoping that he comes back for his other boy."

"One would think."

"I've learned not to do a lot of that kind of thinking in this line of work."

Tom got up and poured two big cups of coffee. He placed one before the policeman. The captain offered his thanks and said, "It's a hell of a deal, a hell of a deal."

Tom had followed the captain and the boy back downtown in his own truck. Two hours later, after 1:00 a.m., Tom and the boy left the station. The boy sat in silence in the truck cab, slumped against the passenger door. It was a dark night. Tom had the vent window open for his cigarette and the larger window cracked. "This shouldn't take too long," he said to the boy, who didn't reply.

Earlier he had identified the young boy's body. The bruises on his face were still plainly evident though they had settled into tones of green and yellow. He saw the face only, but even under the sheet the evidence of new violence bruised the prominent collar bone and crept up the neck. Tom hadn't wanted to imagine the bruises and blood and broken bones that were hidden by the sheet, though he could not help doing so now. The captain had called the funeral home at Tom's insistence. Even as he dialed, the captain had said, "You don't have to do this you know."

"I know."

"The state provides for such things."

"The boy deserves a proper burial," Tom said.

"You could at least wait until the morning."

"I want it over with."

And so he turned the pickup into the gravel back lot of the funeral home. He could hear the gravel crunch and settle beneath the tires.

Tom Matthews had lived in this town all his life, had driven these same streets almost daily, yet he had never entered the doors to the funeral home. One of the oldest houses in town, it hadn't lost any of its Victorian extravagance. He often marveled at the complex trim and scroll work, the carvings over the window and door casings, the intricate angles of its turrets and the ever interrupted line of its architecture. By contrast, this, the backside of the old house, was one flat towering face ascending from the foundation to the roof, one immense clapboarded wall interrupted only by numerous windows, the big double garage door behind which the funeral cars were billeted, and a long wooden staircase, obviously added only in its more recent alteration from home to mortuary. The stairs rose to a single, unprotected door where there now burned an outdoor light.

"You be okay out here for a few minutes?" Tom asked.

The boy nodded.

Tom got out of the truck and extinguished his cigarette. Before he could close the cab door he saw the mortician descending the stairs, a shadow against the wall. The men shook hands somberly and without words at the foot of the stairs, and then Tom followed him to a door adjacent the garage entrance. The mortician fumbled a moment with some keys, angling his position to see their glint in the weak light. He opened the door and reached a light switch. "I apologize for the back door tour," he said. "Normally clients enter through the parlor," he said, his voice a practiced, almost barely audible hum.

"I understand," Tom said.

They entered the garage. Two black limousines stood nose to bumper in the far stall. The hearse alone occupied the near one. The light gleamed on its polished surface and Tom's face reflected back on him in its curtained window.

He followed the mortician through another door and into a narrow hall that smelled of cleaning agents and formaldehyde. Through an open door he glimpsed a metal table and beakers and jars filled with colored liquids. The hall was paneled entirely in dark wood and the carpet, though Tom was uncertain in the poor light, appeared a wine-like red. Through another doorway he saw a large room filled with what resembled church pews, and he was suddenly assaulted with the smell of flowers.

He followed the mortician's back—even now he wore a dark suit coat and dress pants, though, Tom thought, perhaps the coat covered but a nightshirt—down the hall and across a sitting room. "One moment," the man said, indicating a halt with his hand. "Our showroom is this way." He disappeared momentarily and then tiny lights appeared, first like the twinkle of starlight before they flickered to a faint but steady glow dotting a large room and illuminating the polished wood of several caskets. Most were opened to their mid-section to reveal satin fabrics and lace pillows.

"If you will," the mortician said, indicating that Tom should follow him. They passed between an immense white coffin with polished silver handrails and a model embellished throughout with intricate floral carvings in mahogany. Tom had to stay his hand from wanting to touch the rich wood. The mortician turned at a solid black flat-topped casket, pushed aside a velour curtain, and revealed yet another door. There he turned on another set of lights. Tom followed him and entered a small room where five child-sized caskets were displayed side by side on a raised and carpeted platform. "I apologize in advance. This room often disturbs many of our clients," the mortician explained. "Do you have an idea of what you are interested in?"

"Something simple," Tom replied. "As simple as you have."

"Of course," the man said. "I'll get a catalog. If you will excuse me one moment, there are some papers we'll need to complete as well." He stepped out of the room.

Tom stood alone in the room, reluctant to move, for the building was eerily silent. The caskets looked impossibly small. Unlike the room adjacent, none were open. There was one casket set slightly apart from the others, no larger than a bassinette, all in white.

Tom heard a cough from somewhere above him, then the creak of a floorboard or the sound of someone turning heavily in a bed. He remembered watching the mortician descend the outside stairs and wondered at a family living above such a room as the one where he now stood. He heard more coughing and then a child's small cry, another creak followed by steps. Tom turned on his heel. He encountered the mortician in the hall, seeming surprised and disturbed to find Tom other than where he left him. He showed Tom into a small but tidy office where they completed their business.

When Tom stepped back outside the door, he immediately lit a cigarette. The men shook hands, and Tom watched the mortician ascend the steps. He saw a silhouette pass the window next to the door the man entered, then two silhouettes merging. The porch light was extinguished and Tom was left alone in the dark night. Tomorrow he would help bury a boy, a stranger. As he stepped to the pickup, he could hear the sound of his own feet on the gravel.

The boy was gone.

Indeed there was no evidence he was ever there. The same clutter of old receipts and drawings of cabinet configurations and thick carpenter pencils littered the dash. The stale smell of too many cigarettes smoked. There was the faint discoloration of the upholstery of Tom's lone imprint behind the wheel.

He opened the cab door but made no move to get in. A chilly wind passed through Tom's light jacket. He scanned the surrounding yards and hedge-lines. Nothing moved in the night save for the occasional drop of a leaf, and the mountains in the distance seemed impossibly dark, a shade darker still than the night sky. He looked again into the empty pickup cab. Somewhere, he lamented, other fathers and sons navigated the darkness, the brooding lonely circuit trod by men the world had broken and who now waited only for the world to finish them.

The Dark

By Mary Domenico

There are two ways for the girl to survive the night if she wakes up in darkness: she can find someone to sleep with or she can organize her valentines.

It goes without saying that the closet door must be shut and latched before she goes to bed. If the door is open when she startles awake, she must not stare at the black opening, just as she must never stare at the shadowy shapes in the air above her bed or at the thin black gap in the window curtains, because staring makes the faces materialize, the grimacing mouths and menacing hands, or claws, or hooks where hands are missing. Nor is there safety in closed eyes because she cannot help staring into the black canvas of her own eyelids, she cannot prevent seeing what takes form from the scattered shards of light. If she wakes up, she must hold her eyes wide, refuse to blink, because a blink is all it takes, one blink or an inadvertent turn of the head toward the closet, the draperies, or under the bed, but of course she doesn't look down there, ever.

When she was smaller, she could call, "Daddy! Daddy!" He would come into her room in striped pajamas and turn on the light. He'd close the closet door, rearrange the curtains without a black night slit, drop down on his knees to peer under the bed. "There's nothing." Then he'd sit on the edge of the bed and hold her hand, stroke her hair, until she slept. But now if she screams for him, he hollers from his room, "Jesus Christ! Go to sleep! Goddamn it, there's nothing there!"

So, if the girl wakes up and her room is dark and she decides to stay in her bed, chooses not to look for someone to sleep with, then she has to be awake and alert, careful not to look around. Hanging on the back of the chair next to her bed is her valentine bag, the two large pink construction paper hearts stapled together with a strip of red ribbon for a handle. Inside, all the tiny envelopes with her printed name, and the small valentines from her classmates: Be Mine, U R Cool, 2 Good 2 B 4gotten.

Decide on categories: animals, mush, jokes; boys and girls; or small, medium, large, and if there are any that year, the special ones with a little heart that lifts to reveal a piece of hard candy. Remove one envelope from the bag, read the card, place in the right stack. When all of the valentines are assembled on the bed in their neat piles, count each pile and interpret: More from boys than girls, you are popular. More jokes than mush, no one is in love with you. When the round is complete, replace each card in its envelope and put them all back in the bag. Repeat as necessary until the curtains begin to lighten and the room becomes lighter and it is safe. Safe to lie down. Safe to close your eyes. Then sleep. Sleep until your mother comes to wake you. "Rise and shine!"

But if the girl wakes in the night too sleepy to stay alert? If her eyes keep closing? Or if she already made a mistake and glanced at the open closet door or the dark glint of window between the curtains? What if she's been awake, staring into the darkness above her bed until not one, but many faces leer down at her, until she is almost paralyzed, leaden legs and arms sinking into the bed so that soon there will be no escape? What then?

Or maybe the cars drive down her street, flash milky light around her room, searching for her, as her brothers told her would happen. What if she can hear the monsters, the one-eyed cyclops, the crazy man with the knife, all of them, on the other side of the window, ready to crash into her room? What then? Then she must, without hesitation, stand up and jump from her bed to the hallway, run to her brothers' room, find one who will let her crawl in.

She touches his soft cheek, whispers, "Can I sleep with you?"

He holds open the sheet so she can lie next to him on the bottom bunk, pulls the covers over her shoulders, up to her neck. He turns on his side, facing her, with his yeasty boy smell. It is dark here, too, but this brother is big. He snuggles against her back, curls around her, puts his arm over her and slips his fingers inside her panties, inside of her. She feels his warm breath in little puffs in her hair. She is safe. She closes her eyes and sleeps. Until her mother comes in. "Rise and shine!"

———•———

The twenty-year-old girl lives by herself in downtown Denver at the top of a dilapidated Victorian, and when the cab pulls up to the curb in the middle of the night, the house is entirely dark, the windows black and shiny, Gothic. From the front seat, without even looking at her, the driver must sense her hesitation because, as if she'd asked, he says, "I'll walk you." He turns up the volume, leaves the radio on, the sounds as they approach the front stoop are a combination of their shoes scuffing on the small stones of broken concrete and the scratchy electrical buzz from the dash. She unlocks the front door, reaches inside for the light. When nothing happens, the cab driver reaches around her to toggle the switch himself, she smells cigarette smoke, his arm in a green canvas jacket brushes across her chest, and there is in this motion of his arm touching her breasts a signal of sorts, her vulnerability is communicated, along with her fear of the dark stairs, just as when he enters the hallway with her there is silent agreement, or perhaps more precisely a relinquishment on her part, but in any case it is settled that he, the cab driver, will come with her up the narrow stairs to her apartment.

Through the small second floor landing window comes enough milky light for her to see her own shadow creeping along the wallpaper, across peeling seams and the small dingy pattern of flowers, the bulk of her body and her head distorted, too large, unfamiliar, but when she reaches a hand to smooth down her hair, the man touches the small of her back with his fingertips and she stumbles. Old wood creaks.

She uses the key in the handle, in the deadbolt. She pushes open the door and she and the cab driver enter. She stands to one side, waiting in her buttoned blue peacoat, wallet in hand to pay him, while he fumbles along the wall for the switch to the living room fixture, two bare bulbs that glare on the bare walls and the bare floor. She waits on this one spot, near the door, while he walks through the four rooms. She watches him, a short, muscular man with a mop of red hair graying at the sides, watches him open her broom closet and go into her bathroom, hears him slide back the shower curtain.

"There's nothing," he says, as if she'd asked, and then, when she hands him the ten dollar bill, "I do want to make love to you," as if they'd been having a conversation and been interrupted, as if he were picking up an earlier stream of words now that he'd done this for her, this searching of her apartment. "I do want to make love to you," not a question to which she need respond, not a question at all, but a statement reinforcing his intention, and he fucks her the same way, with confidence, with force, like he belongs there, as if all had been decided in advance, in the normal flow of things between them, and it is this assuredness on his part that makes her assume that yes, she did agree, she must have, or this would not be happening, this man on top of her, inside her.

Her bedroom, a rickety third floor balcony enclosed with leaky windows, is at the front of the house and from the street below she hears his radio, the broken mechanical voice of the woman dispatcher speaking in code. She listens to taxi numbers and street addresses through his moaning climax, and his parting words, "I have to go work. I'll be back."

A shaft of light from the living room shines across the bottom half of her bed, illuminating her bare white legs and bare white feet. She sits, straightens the ransacked sheet with flat hands, then lies back, pulls the covers over her shoulders, up to her neck. On the pillow, his cigarette breath, on the sheet, his stale skin. She turns from the dark windows, curls up with her knees to her chest, holds herself. And then she closes her eyes and sleeps. The girl sleeps.

Provenance

By Carol Samson

1.

My grandmother bore no flowers. They found me secondhand in Huerfano County. I always thought of them, driving north through the flat prairie, all seabed, the foundry in the distance, rising on the dry land like a black steamship with tall smoke stacks. The orphanage in the town center had a pond and mallard ducks. I sat by that pond, a spindly thing, all elbows and a nose like a beak. They asked me what I cared about most in the world, and I said, "Quiet places." I told them I'd like a room where I could sit by myself and listen to my mind. I saw the man smile. He was a spindly thing, too, his smile only a thin crease in his face. He had on a white straw hat with a blue ribbon band and a wintry kind of suit that looked like it was the only one he had. We sat by the pond. I brushed a brown feather I found over my knees. I closed my eyes and brushed my eyelashes. I lay back on the grass and stared at the sun. They told me they would stop by the next week.

2.

My grandmother told me everything is secondhand, I should remember that. Every pie or cut flower or story started somewhere else and surrendered itself. "Is that bird feather yours?" she'd asked. "Are your words yours or are you borrowing them?" I liked this idea of hand-me-down everythings. I would stand and watch her in the bakery that they ran, white flour powdering her hair, her thick arms rolling out the dough like cloth and folding the edges of the breakfast buns so as to hold the cherry jam or peach or raspberry in the center. "I learned this from my mother," she'd say. "Secondhand." And she would pass the fresh rolls over the counter to young mothers already tired of the morning or to railroad men just off shift. She'd bag them in brown paper. "Secondhand," she'd say to me as she took the dollar bills. She even said that was why I should call her "grandmother." She said there was a mother somewhere, not here, and eventually whatever that word "mother" means to that woman had to stay with her, so her title would be "grandmother" as in Eve, as in curiosity.

My grandfather, the spindly man, was called Jake. He ran the bakery, getting up at 3 a.m. to make the bread and doughnuts, letting my grandmother make the Napoleons and the Lady Baltimores and the butter cream icings for wedding cakes in the afternoon. After lunch he would walk me down to the river. I was only seven when I came to them, toting a tied-up box with all my earthly possessions from the orphanage, and Jake held my hand gently as if I would break. When we took walks together, he never said much. He just listened to the stream. Years later when he died, a quiet death, an aneurysm of some sort, we buried him in the cemetery in a plot closest to the river. He told me once that rivers merely cycle and return. I thought he meant they go up and become clouds and rain down. He didn't. He meant they circle in time, moving all over the earth to come back. You can, he told me, step in the same river twice.

After dinner my grandmother would crochet, her hands like wild birds. I would sit beside her and watch the patterns emerge, cabled thumbs and chains of lace, like legions of memory at her command. Sometimes we would watch Lawrence Welk and that man with the accordion. It was the late 1950s and the dancers swirled or jitterbugged or waltzed and soap bubbles filled the back of the stage. Sometimes we would just take an evening stroll down the main street of town with its Duckwalls and its one bar and café and the movie theater and pharmacy at the corner where the road turns to Alamosa. I liked the large plate glass windows of the dress shops and the way the car salesman drove new Fords into a main street building and put them on display. I liked the quiet, the way the windows of the shops reflected off of one another, the way I could see how the mannequins in flowered dresses on one side of the street appeared to be standing beside the 1958 two-tone Ford cars on the other.

Sometimes I think you know a town better when it isn't yours. If it's yours, you stop looking and you miss the cornices with Huerfano County A. 1904 D. on the courthouse or the arched red sign of the Fireside Café or even the handprints in the cement of the main street dated 1931. Sometimes I think my grandmother understood that we must stand witness, secondhand witness, to see anything. Each Sunday she showed me Red Ryder cartoons in the Sunday newspaper, Red Ryder and his horse and his friend the Indian boy. One summer Red Ryder came to town for the parade. That day she dressed me in blue jeans with the bottoms rolled and a white shirt with pearl buttons and a red cowboy hat and a beaded Indian belt she bought in Santa Fe on her honeymoon. She took me down to the courthouse lawn, and there he was, the real thing, a good man, a smiling magazine-type model man. But I had seen the other one, the cartoon one with the square jaw and the horse with a wild eye, and I knew it was just as good. She took a picture of me there with her box camera. I was standing next to the Indian boy, Red Ryder is behind me but his head is cut off, and I can see she had curled my hair in sausage curls and pressed the hat down and tied it on with the white strings. Even in black and white you can tell the hat is red. And if you look closely, you'll see how my grandmother's shadow cuts into the picture. It rises at my feet and overwhelms me as I smile into the sun. In the picture her shadow covers half of my forehead where we seem to share one eye.

3.

My room was yellow. We lived over the bakery, Spanish Peaks Bakery, and I looked out over the side street that led to the school. She put a desk by the window and bookshelves beside it on the wall, and she lined the shelves with used copies of Nancy Drew and Cherry Ames and a volume of poems by Robert Louis Stevenson with a marker by "The Lamplighter." We were close to the school, but she walked me there every day. At three o'clock she'd be there near the fence waiting, watching the kids who lived miles away board the orange bus that went to La Veta and Ft. Garland. On a hot August day, she sent Jake with me to Pueblo to buy school shoes. He took me by the hand to the Buster Brown store where they let me stand with my feet in this machine so I could see my spindly toes turn green like sticks in the radiated light. Jake always picked sturdy shoes, the sturdier the better. "Choose quality," he said to me as he tucked the box under his arm. I remember sturdy red shoes with thick soles and plaid laces. I remember my grandmother's face when she opened the box. She had expected black patent leather shoes, girl's shoes to go with white socks. "Oh, Jake," she said with disappointment, "these won't do. They're brogans." Brogans. I did not know what that meant. I said I liked them. She said they were going back. The only time I saw them fight was that time over shoes.

I thought about her voice when I was ten and the shoe man came. His name was Mitchell, and he drove a used school bus filled with boxes of shoes. We didn't have to go to Pueblo, the shoe man came to us. He stopped in front of the library in August and in May. He stepped down the stairs and stood in the sun in a starched shirt with blue suspenders and grey trousers. He stretched and wiped his brow and shifted his back muscles. He reached back and drew out his suit jacket and put it on even in the hot sun. I could tell he was a clever man, a man from somewhere in the north, Cheyenne maybe, or Ft. Collins, somewhere with cottonwood trees, north. He had a route. He'd taken the seats out of the bus and replaced them with shelves. He kept one row of seats for customers to sit and try on the shoes, and he had work boots and black Mary Janes and baby shoes and thick walking boots with laces of every color.

He had cowboy boots and spectator pumps. He had large metal gadgets to measure the toes, and he had a smile that said he'd met you before, even if he hadn't.

I was helping my grandmother with the vanilla pudding when she turned by chance and saw him out the window with his bus. She knew him, I could tell. Her face went still, her eye cold.

"Mitchell," was all she said.

"Do you know him?"

"Did once—a long time ago. He hasn't been around for years."

"Does he sell brogans?" I asked, saying the word, borrowing it.

"He'll sell you whatever you want."

She turned back to the pudding, to the Napoleons. I watched the man tip his hat to the passersby. He had dark black hair and eyes that matched. He was not spindly. He seemed to care about every person who crossed his path.

By my count, Mitchell was in town for only three hours, fanning himself with his hat, smiling, then closing the bus and drifting to the café for dinner. Thin sliced beef, mashed potatoes, I imagined, with buttery green peas. Then he walked up the street, stepped into the bus, ground the clutch, and headed north to make it to Stem Beech or Colorado City before night. I watched him at the window, memorizing the thick oil of his head, even the sweat moons under his arms. My grandmother never looked up all afternoon. She made profiteroles as if she thought there would be a run on them.

In the evening I asked her, "You knew him when he was a young man?" but she did not look up from her crochet, her hands just moved and the squares of yellow and blue came out like ordered windows. Jake was asleep. He went to bed around 7:30 to get up by 3 a.m. for the bread. He never heard our evening talks.

"Yes."

"Handsome?"

"Yes."

"He make you laugh?"

"Not me, in particular."

"Who, then?"

"Someone. Blond girl."

"Friend of yours?"

"Not so much."

"He sell her what she wanted? Anything she wanted?" I borrowed her words.

"You could say that." And she put down the yarn and turned on the Lawrence Welk show. She did not look my way. "Goodness, those bubbles, those bubbles," was all she said.

Her reticence stayed with me. I'd see him twice a year only, Mitchell. He never seemed to age, but I knew he had to, all that driving, all those plates of café mashed potatoes. I saw him about eight times altogether, the last time in the week before Jake died, one Sunday afternoon in May. After the funeral my grandmother and I sat by the kitchen table. The people had gone. We had casseroles with green beans and mushroom soup lined up on the counter and foil-wrapped lasagnas and loaves of homemade bread, someone feeling that we probably couldn't make it ourselves for a while.

My grandmother didn't cry. It was if she felt we'd just borrowed Jake a while from some big lending library, like we're all on some layaway plan. She sat at the table and sipped her coffee with milk. She looked out the window at the back of our lot that faced the school. She reached up once in a while and patted the top of her hair as if to tame the humidity that made it lift away from her face.

"When I'm gone," she said. "You can tell them that Mitchell killed him."

"The shoe man?" I couldn't believe it. "Mitchell wasn't even here. Jake died in his chair watching some program on lions."

"It was Mitchell just the same," she said. "Mitchell. You can tell them after I die,"

4.

What I know is that the base of life, if there is one, is memory. Sometimes nowadays I like to watch that program *Antiques Roadshow* because, I think, it proves my point every Wednesday from 7 to 8 p.m. My grandmother liked it too. She lived well into her eighties and we would sit in her living room on an overstuffed couch she bought as a newlywed in 1948. She liked the odd childrens' banks of heavy iron with figures of firemen and fire brigade horses. She liked the turquoise glaze vases from Van Briggle Pottery because she knew that that Van Briggle man came to Colorado for a tuberculosis cure in 1900. It wasn't the items, the dragonfly brooches or the German stuffed bears with glass eyes, that intrigued her so much as the stories of dying aristocrats who passed paintings on to scullery maids or Vermont ladies who found that their cherry pie plate dated from the Revolutionary War. My grandmother said that provenance is the only meaning, the pie plate was just clay unless you knew who touched it.

I suppose I agree with her to an extent, and I think that provenance, the original owners, may make a difference, but in the end it is desire that presses us to collect things. I say it is all desire, surfaces that pull us in like trout. Somehow, I say, our eye meets a pattern that we recognize inside of us, the twist of a branch, the geometry of a tile, the red color of a jewel, and the object replicates the abstraction already there, inside. We see an inner self turned out in surface design. It is not aesthetic or historic or intellectual. It is a moment of desire, a feeling of water running in the self, a wallowing. In the end, I say, we collect what we are.

5.

I only learned the story secondhand. My grandmother never told me. I learned it from the mother of a friend at school, this tale of how Mitchell killed Jake. It did, as my grandmother hinted, involve a blond girl. Her name was Herta. She was Latvian, all yellow-white hair and cheekbones that made promontories under her eyes. Her uncle brought her here days after the war when relatives found her. She was only seventeen when she arrived, but she had stood witness to the hanging of her husband at the hands of the Nazis. The soldiers made her watch him die, forced her to make memory of their power. Her uncle sent money to his brother, and the family somehow managed to get her out of Latvia to Walsenburg where they ran a pharmacy. Herta worked there with her cousins. She spoke no English when she came, but her eyes were a source of consolation for everyone in town after the war. None of us, everyone in town would say, would ever know the suffering that Herta knew, watching a young boy, suspended like a catalpa pod, swinging in the light breeze, his feet moving in small gravitational circles.

Jake was a devoted disciple, age eighteen years, at the pharmacy. He bought band-aids and aspirin that he didn't need. Sometimes in spring, he would take her hand-picked bouquets of lilacs. "Purple stars," he would tell her, speaking slowly. "Constellations." I wondered if he ever walked with her by the river or if he taught her, as he did me, about the magnetism of the sun when we found our separate spots and lay down on our backs on the bank, our arms stretched like birds, when we let the yellow sun fade into us and let the Earth give us her magnetism. That's what Jake called it, "getting our magnetism." Sometimes I hope he didn't teach her that. I hope he saved it just for me.

My grandmother watched the courting, watched it all. She was not married to Jake then, but she cared about him. She worked in the Duckwall's behind the counter, and she would see him go by the window, lilacs in his hand going one way, pharmacy sacks coming back. Sometimes on her break she would cross the street just to stand in the pharmacy and listen to the townspeople honor Herta in their own way, speaking slowly and loudly, asking for cold elixirs or cough syrup as if the words were new in this world. If Herta chanced to come to Duckwall's to buy yarn in winter or flowered material from the bolts in the back in summer, my grandmother merely took the yarn or the fabric, tapped in the price on the cash register and took her money. No funny words. No smile. No field of grace. My grandmother merely noted the girl's brogans, the sound thick leather soles made as Herta went out the door.

When summer came that year, everyone could see Jake was smitten. My grandmother knew it, too. She would see him leave his father's bakery at 5 p.m. and cross the street to wait for her so he could walk her home. Quiet boy. Latvian girl. Lilacs or wild flowers. The girl, looking down at the flowers, her head bowed to their color. The young man walking at her elbow, his eyes looking defensively ahead to some future time lined in the cement.

6.

I have these albums, black pages with black and white pictures with the white ruffled edges. I have pictures of people I do not know. She left them to me. They intrigue me with their momentary opaque worlds, faces looking at me, or rather at somebody I have become in the moment I look. Faces that make me into the gazer, the picture taker. In them I see life in bits, like daubs of paint. I read the albums like a text of posed worlds, for in these old books, there are no candid or random tellings. People stand in knowing states, assured that the world is what they know it to be. There they are at holiday tables, at vacation sights with signs telling the elevation, at tombstones. And they are glued into the books in sequence, fixed with white or black photo corners, bits of secured time. They age in the turning of these pages and they disappear. Even the ones who did the gluing disappear. And the album comes into the hands of relatives or neighbors or *Antiques Roadshow* sorts who make it into history or economics. All that assurance in the eyes of the lady in the belted 1940s dress or the bride in the white satin, all that freshness twisted, like a sugar beet in the ground, by the scrutiny of the unknowing.

Here is how I see one picture I never saw. It is a grey day, in black and white, but you can tell it is summer. Mitchell is there, ten years younger, 1947 this time, smiling. He is standing by his bus with all the shoes, leaning on the hood and wearing a light grey suit and suspenders and a bow tie of a dark color, perhaps a navy blue. The sun is at noon, at peak, no shadows. All is quiet, nothing moves except one haunting white-haired girl in a flowery grey skirt, in black and white, butter yellow with green flowers in truth, and she lifts her chin to laugh at something Mitchell has just said. She has on a white blouse, open at the throat, and the sun is hot, and her face lifts to him like it would to an altar figure in her church. There is no album picture like this, but I suspect my grandmother made the image often in her mind. Her silences passed it all to me. Then, as I see it, they were gone. He touched her face, maybe. He spoke quietly, the way he might gentle a skittish horse. He said words like "Denver. Cheyenne. Laramie. Yellowstone." And the girl who had watched her passionate young husband, feet and arms tied back, swinging in the air like a pendulum, like a flour sack pulling downward, decided to let herself know unbridled freedom. She decided to let herself out of the cage, to go away from the faces gazing at the windows. The way I see it she got in the bus. They went north. He had a route. He would take her where the cottonwood trees stretched their long, turgid roots, where water was easy. He would dress her up, give her red leather shoes, take her to restaurants with singers at the microphone, call her "Doll" like those men did in the movies. It was desire, you see. She had stepped in the same river twice.

7.

My grandmother believed a person could die of a broken heart. She said that at her wedding to Jake, in 1948, she had taken his hands at the Episcopal church and his hands were like dead fish, cold, cold. He had smiled at her, she said, but she could see that his mind was somewhere else and the smile was more of a "thank you" than a happiness smile. She said they both knew that she had rescued a shy and spindly man from a life of loneliness. Of course, she told me, she had planned this moment, making Lady Baltimores and Napoleons in her mother's kitchen and taking them down to the bakery for him to taste, watching his eyes as he bit into her éclairs, brushing powdered sugar from his mouth as he consumed her delicate sponges with vanilla cream between the layers. She seduced him with fillings, raspberry and lemon. She courted him with mousses lathered between chocolate slabs of cake. Trust pudding, she told me. Trust pudding.

She got him secondhand. I have the picture, black and white. She is posed by a rosebush, and her suit, by my guess, is light blue. Her face is round under her hat, her hair trying to pull out from underneath it. She is holding a bouquet of wildflowers, standing beside her awkward groom who is squinting at the picture taker. It must be noon. There are no shadows. The sun is not in his face, yet he is squinting. I see no magnetism here.

But when I consider Mitchell with that Herta by his side, I can hear their laughter in that bus as he teaches her the names of cities on the road: Stem Beech and Rye and Longmont and Windsor and Greeley and Eton and Virginia Dale. They ride with her sitting on the customer seat in the front and the boxes of shoes shifting and swaying against each other. Sometimes he pulls off a dirt road somewhere by Colorado City and they make love in the bus, lying on a quilt on the floor. Sometimes he takes her to dinner for steaks at restaurants on Colfax in Denver where women in long red gowns sing songs like "Shrimp Boats Is A'comin, There's Dancing Tonight." Sometimes they splurge on a motel, buying only store-bought bread and cheese and wine to have in their room. And they have a system. When they arrive at a point on the route, he lets her off on the edge of town or at a park with picnic tables, telling her he'll be back in just three hours. In small towns, he tells her, it is better that he show up alone. He needs to make the customers laugh, he says. Flirt a bit when you come right down to it, he says. She nods. She understands. She sits on the park bench in the shade, tracing her finger along the flowers on her skirt. She is happy. She listens to the birds. She watches the wind touch the wheat stalks. She hums songs about shrimp boats. Sometimes she closes her eyes and, suddenly, the boy she used to know is swinging from the tree.

Of course, they stopped coming to Walsenburg for a few years. Mitchell cut it from the route. The only school buses down the main street had farm children looking from the windows. Parents had to drive to Pueblo or Trinidad to get school shoes. No one knew what happened to them. Her uncle never said her name. People started talking normally at the pharmacy, ordering ear drops and leaving. Jake got up every morning at 3 a.m. and made doughnuts. Each day he made more doughnuts than he made words.

8.

There is a white-edged picture of my grandmother and Jake and me coming out of the orphanage. I'm holding my box of things, tied shut. My hair is in pigtails. I am seven years old. They are five years married. Over the steps of the old brick dormitory are the words, "We are bound as children dancing." I remember that, in the car as we passed Stem Beech on the way to Walsenberg, my grandmother turned to the back seat where I sat, wearing blue shorts and a white blouse, and she said, "Huerfano County. That's where we live. Huerfano, pronounced 'Wherefano.' Means 'orphan' in Spanish." I watched the blue peaks rising on the side of the road. I saw a few stray cows, a pinto horse, but mostly sagebrush, dry land. We passed the steamship that was the ironworks and sixty miles down the road turned off to Walsenburg, the road rising past the Hill Top Motel of white adobe and down past the middle school and stucco houses and county seat, across the railroad tracks to the bakery. There is another picture of us in front of the bakery on that same day. I don't know who took the picture, but there at our feet sits a dog, a white dog, in black and white. I would learn, in time, that he was the town wanderer. Everyone fed him. Stray dog, probably. Huerfano.

9.

She came back on a Thursday in the fall, sixteen years after she had left, 1963. I was in high school and on counter duty at the bakery on that afternoon in October. The air was finally autumn cool, leaves were slipping from the few trees in town. The Greyhound bus pulled in and stopped, and I watched as she got off, a woman I had never seen before. She was a bloated thing, filled with water, her face puffy and red and unwell. She wore an old wool coat and a cotton dress, and her shoes were odd, old fashioned, sort of 1940 pumps, red. Her hair was white, pure white, and thinning around her face. I watched her. I was the only one there. She picked up a black suitcase and walked to the pharmacy. I felt this chill, I remember. She was otherworldly, dragging that suitcase like some ghostly silt of a thing.

Her uncle took her in, nursed her, gave her back the color in the white ashen face. She commenced to work at the pharmacy again. My grandmother only said, "So, Herta's come back from her travels." I knew my grandmother went to the pharmacy for more than one reason. Everybody did, buying St. Joseph's aspirin and bandaids and toe pads for corns. I suspect she took time to examine the ruin this woman had become. She was so thick, her fingers larger than the rings she wore, a turquoise stone on one hand, a silver band on the other, her dress belt cinched at the last hole, her blue eyes like small blue plums pressed in dough. I suspect my grandmother just handed her the pills and paid. And, one day, as the winter snows came and she had adjusted to the haunted soul who sold medicines, my grandmother held her bag with cough syrup in one hand and her change in the other. The snow whirling past the window, she looked into the woman's eyes and said, "Jake's dead," and walked away, a bell jangling at the door. I suspect she was stern in her pronouncement about the dead made to the almost dead.

Now, this is secondhand, but the town said that Mitchell kept Herta only as long as she was pretty. The town said he wore her out with babies that they abandoned across the western states. Babies cannot live in school buses and motels, he told her; and she had to agree. They say he kept her in that bus like a Rapunzel in a tower for years. Then he set her down somewhere in Kansas where she lived alone, a beauty in decay, until her arms thickened and her body filled with juices and gravity pulled at her breasts and stomach. Then, I suspect, she felt that something was wrong inside her and she came back to set it right. Everyone in town said it was an infection of the womb, of that vulnerable and desirous place inside her where she dropped babies like a ewe. I said it was probably the heart. In towns like ours, it's usually the heart. Whatever part it was, she kept going, shuffling around filling prescriptions in old house slippers with run-down heels, her feet thick, her ankles and legs all one column. She was focused and efficient. She was all white, her skin, her hair, her blouse and her pharmacist's coat, but we all thought she was getting better.

It was about the time that I graduated from high school that the chain store, Safeway with an inside pharmacy, moved in on the edge of town, and her uncle felt he must give up his drugstore. She said she would help him as he helped her. She would make his store a cottage industry, a thrift store, a collectibles shop. And so, as I watched, she became a paradox. It was odd, I thought, to fill the shop with things nobody wanted, white elephants. Odd to try to make the castaway item significant, desirous. She would go down the Walsenburg alleys and find abandoned things. She would take the bus to Pueblo to go to the Salvation Army. She would gather anything the library abandoned at its yearly sale. And she filled that room that was once the pharmacy. She had old Christmas ornaments and coffee thermos bottles and glass cats and toasters. She had costume jewelry and fiesta ware plates and floor lamps with glass bowl tops. She had horseshoes and an elk head with glass eyes. She had old pillows made of cheap satin with the state of Nevada stenciled on the center.

And we all knew she sat in the corner, breathing from her spongey lungs and waiting for someone to enter the big dark place to buy a ceramic dog or a straw hat or a cotton handkerchief with pink roses. Mostly, though, you could tell she just watched us over the counter, over the abandoned things. I could feel her on my skin. I knew she was there behind the jewelry cases where she kept the gold casket boxes made of pot metal, the Indian necklaces and beaded belts. As I circled, looking at the plastic flowers or the silverware in shoe boxes, her lungs pulled hard in the dust, in the musky odors of the shadowed room. In the darkness of her shop, she had stopped wearing white. She chose silken black dresses with shoulder pads, loose in the bodice, belted, the style of the 1940s. I do not know where she got them. And she started to dye her hair a sheeny black to match the dress, in time forgetting to freshen the color, letting it grow white at the roots like a field of winter snow.

Once I bought a small plate from her. It said "Czechoslovakia" on the back. I saw her eyes were watering, the pupils becoming foggy. She wore no spectacles. Perhaps, I thought, light hurt her eyes.

"Cookie plate." That was the only phrase I ever said to her.

She nodded. She wrapped it in newspaper and put it in brown paper tied with string.

10.

The box under my bed all these years is wrapped in brown paper and tied with string. It is the box I carried out of Pueblo that day long ago, the box I am holding in the picture with the stray dog. It was wrapped that way when they handed it to me and for a while my grandmother placed it high on a shelf in the linen closet. One day she took it down and said, "Perhaps we should open this now. It could tell you who you are." I said, "I know who I am." She put the box under my bed.

I am told there is a theory in physics, something called Schrödinger's cat. The theory says that given a box with a radioactive element, a Geiger counter, a flask of poison, and a cat, and given the possibility that the element might decay and set off the counter that would spill the poison and kill the cat, you must always assume the cat to be dead and alive. You must allow for the possibility of the particle or the cat being in two states at one time.

I understand that theory. Whatever is in that box is dead and alive to me until I open it. It is a collection, perhaps a pair of baby shoes, a letter in some language I do not know, a confession of desire. Perhaps there is a photograph with white edges, a red ribbon for my hair, a golden ring. When I think of the box, I know only possibility.

We fill our wombs as best we can.

The owl, they say, was a baker's daughter.

A Bird, Yabba

By Alison Flowers

My American mother knew I didn't like feeling foreign, so she would let me order the school cafeteria's food once a week. I tried to look extra American on those days. I'd wear some Nikes and a stiff ball cap that I'd tried all week to break in, and I'd order chocolate milk and drink it slowly, savoring its richness. On an "American" day, my dad, or *Yabba* as I called him, would pick me up from school. He'd pull up in our Benz, his first car and the only car he had ever really driven. In Palestine, his family couldn't afford a car, and even after years in America, he still hadn't been able to afford one, surviving on student meal plans and grants for tuition. Once he got the Benz at the age of thirty, after finally benefiting from years of biochemical studies, he didn't want to ding it up, so he drove it carefully—almost mechanically—which gave the kids at school even more material with which to make fun of me. I was the rich kid and the Arab kid, and they called my family "a bunch of terrorists." Every day after school, Yabba asked me about how my day had gone and about what I had learned. One time, I asked him a question that Mrs. Landers had used that morning as a prompt for our Arts and Crafts class. I was eight years old.

"Yabba, if you could be any animal in the whole wide world, what would you be?"

"A bird, Yabba."

Because he was my dad, he called me the Arabic word for "Dad," too. It's the Arab way of referring to family members.

"How come a bird, Yabba?"

He turned to me and looked me in the eye, and I paid attention as he answered me. At that time, his Arabic accent was still thick.

"You know, Jonathan, when I was like you, I did not have shoes and clothing that was so nice. My shoes were full of sand because I sold newspapers after school. And when I would stand there, I would look at the sky and see some birds fly. The birds are free, Yabba. The birds can fly over the checkpoints and over the mountains of dirt."

I could never imagine my father in any position of vulnerability. To me, he was a great man—a successful, charismatic businessman who took frequent trips to dine with Saudi Arabian emirs to discuss biochemical technology. He gave lectures all over the world. I could never picture him being pushed around as a boy, selling combs or ice cream or postcards to the white tourists like he did in Golgotha. Piles of dirt and intimidation could not stop him.

My dad liked to practice his English when he told me bedtime stories. I loved the one about how he met my mom in a chemistry class at Wichita State University during a spring semester. When my dad proposed to my mom, he had to use the tagline that they had "good chemistry" from the start. I laughed at this joke even before I understood what it meant because Yabba thought it was so funny. He was a teaching assistant, difficult for the Americans to understand. My mom told me that back then his accent used to be even more slurred, like Arabic, and so unpredictable in its rhythm, like a good jazz. My mom was from a small town outside of Wichita, and she had never met or frankly even heard of a Palestinian. In fact, she thought Palestinians were Jews from Israel. I think she'd admit she didn't know what he was and that she never cared. She still seems to love his "sweet" clumsiness and thoughtfulness. He once told her she was the most beautiful Western woman he'd ever met, blonde and fair. Lightness for his darkness.

"And, believe me, I know!" he would tell us over dinner, wildly raising and waving his finger. "When I saw your mother for the first time, I made an exclamation, Jonathan. I said '*Ma'shallah!*'"

I knew what this expression meant because at home our speech was always spiced with lots of Arabic. *Ma'shallah*: *Thanks be to God.*

Yabba would also tell me bedtime stories about their "creative" dates. They'd find a soft spot of land in a wheat field and watch the airplanes at Wichita airport take off and land into the panoramic Kansas sunsets. Free entertainment. Three months after they met, at the Wichita Justice of the Peace, they were married and moved into the modest apartment where I was born a few years later. On their first anniversary, my dad returned home from a long day at work and school to find a freshly baked cake resting on the stovetop.

My mom popped around the corner and said, "I didn't even use a box, Hasan! I made it from scratch!"

He didn't understand, but he turned to her and rubbed her back and answered, "Well, one day we will be able to afford the box stuff, *habibti.*" *My dear, my darling.*

Growing up, my parents and I always ate Arabic food: *malfoof, tabouleh, hummus*. At home, I loved it. But whenever I ate my leftovers at school, I became the funny Arab kid again. The kids made faces at my food and dared each other to sniff it.

"It's just *makloobeh*," I informed them, shrugging and pretending that it wasn't my absolute favorite Arabic dish, especially the eggplant slices, a deep purple in color and taste. The kids called it slime. My face grew both hot and cold.

When I was a freshman in high school, I finally found one friend named Rascal who was willing to try the "ethnic shit." He liked it, but didn't admit it in front of our football buddies. Rascal and I never did talk about that evening when he showed up at our front door, tapping our ornate, gold knocker that my dad picked up in Jerusalem. I opened the door and tried not to notice his red eyes and large pupils. We made him our special guest. We cooked a full Arabic meal. My mom had even made *kanaffe* that night, a delicately prepared dessert with soft, milky cheese underneath sweet, shredded dough and topped with a sticky, orange-colored syrup. We served him our best, but by Monday morning at football practice, he kept his distance, and after practice, he used a starchy locker room towel to make fun of the *keffiyeh*, the Arafat-style head covering that some Arabs wear, but not anyone in my family.

———•———

When I was in high school, my dad's chemical company really took off. It seemed like once my parents finally made money—real, sweat-earned money—they would never settle for anything meager. They began to purchase better things and soon practically everything we owned was big. Our SUVs. Our company plants and laboratories. The farm tractor for our cattle. The stables for our horses. Even now, years later, my parents' house still gets bigger and bigger, sprawling wider over their property.

The summer after I graduated from high school, my dad took my mother and me to Israel to meet my Palestinian family for the first time. I officially met all my relatives, but I already knew them from bedtime stories and a few pocket-creased pictures. My cousins and I quickly overcame our initial shyness, and soon I found myself in their kitchen smoking *arghileh*, or *hookah*, the water pipes that people use to smoke flavored tobacco. They had to coax me to take the first puff.

"Jon-a-than! Jon-a-than!" they chanted.

One of my cousins, Najeeb, whispered something in the ear of the only English-speaking cousin, Nadia. Her eyes lit up, and she laughed before relaying the message, working out the translation in her mind.

"Jeeb has said, 'Do not be like a white American!'"

I cracked up as I examined my fair complexion, wondering why their teasing didn't bother me so much. I ran my fingers over the mouthpiece attached to the golden, steaming contraption.

"Jon-a-than! Jon-a-than!"

I took a gulp of the smoke and didn't even cough. It tasted like the lemons that grow in Jerusalem—patchy, yet plentiful, like sunlight. As casually as possible, I allowed the citrus smoke to slowly escape my parted lips. It almost perfectly matched the color of their concrete walls. It swirled into the air and mixed with the smoke that my cousins were emitting as we talked, relaxing in the heavy aromas. The heaviness reminded me of how my parents used to smoke cigarettes when I was young. They were young then themselves. Before I found out at school that smoking was bad, I loved to watch the gray clouds distort the air. I watched my dad's olive-skinned hand bring the cigarette to his wide lips. He inhaled as though it fed him and cloaked him with warmth, as though his smoky breath were a result of cold weather. I remember thinking that his long, white cigarettes had a fluorescent quality about them, like light sabers cutting through the gray smoke. My mom had her own cigarettes that produced another scent altogether different from my dad's. Her cigarettes smelled American somehow, like her, and my dad's smelled like he did—exotic, foreign, and spicy.

No matter how old I was, Yabba told me stories about what he was like when he was my age. When I was eight, my dad bought me the new Reebok Pumps. When Yabba was eight, he wore shoes handed down from two older brothers. He had to cram his feet into the leather and walk on crumpled toes because his brothers' feet were much smaller than his. When I was sixteen, I played Babe Ruth baseball. When Yabba was sixteen, he dug a hole and slept in it, covering himself with the dirt to stay warm during the Six Day War, "a total misery," as he says. Because of his stories, I could never go through life without knowing what it had been like for him. During college, I followed in my father's footsteps and studied biochemistry. I was so nervous the first day of class, which must have been a fraction of the nervous feeling of possibility and opportunity—that faint, sweet whiff of success—that must have overwhelmed my father as he boarded the plane at the Tel Aviv Yaffo airport to come to America. He was seventeen and had finally sold enough knick-knacks to Israeli soldiers to buy a ticket. They always gave him a very fair price, he told me. One time a soldier smiled, patted him on the back, and bought everything my dad was selling. All forty-eight postcards, all sixty-seven combs. Yabba didn't know whether to hug him or punch him or just cry. He didn't understand. That day, he said he had to take the long way home because the shortcut was blocked off again for security.

He told me how strange everything in America, *everything*, was to him, "an upside-down universe," he said, pronouncing it yoo-nee-vairse. Everything was so different to him. He laughed and laughed the first time someone called him a foreigner.

"No, *you* are the foreigner!" he had said.

Unlike my dad, I was treated pretty normally in college. Cafeteria food and twin beds seemed a little foreign to me because I was used to better food and a bigger bed. But for Yabba, American college life was like a VIP experience. From the moment someone from Mid-American Nazarene College, the only university that would accept his application, picked him up at the airport, he felt like a king. Other students thought the cafeteria food was "nasty" (I still crack up when my dad says that word), so he was kind of embarrassed to admit that he liked the food—loved it, actually. His pride wasn't great enough to keep him from being the first in line, though, and he was elated when he learned it was okay to get back in line for seconds or thirds or fourths, in his case. He never missed a meal, he never wasted food, and he never left until he was very, very full.

These stories of my father would fill my imagination as I stared at my dorm room ceiling late at night. I imagined him twenty-five years ago, warm and stuffed, looking at his ceiling and thinking of what his mother and father and sisters and brothers might be doing at that moment. When I thought of my own parents, I knew they would be well fed and safe, but Yabba could never be sure. He would hope it had been a good day in Bethlehem without curfews and too much harassment. I would imagine him as a boy during mealtime with his family, as they crowded around a table, contained in their concrete walls, the afternoon rain sliding through the crack between the moistened, molding roof and the jagged walls. His mother would be preparing fresh mint tea, ripping leaves off the plant in strong palmfuls, the sweet aroma hanging in the dampness. If they were lucky, it'd be a meat day, maybe some roasted lamb, and they'd go "refugee style," what I call their method of using *khubiz*, bread, to scoop up the braised cauliflower and carrots. When I visited the first time, the surroundings distracted me from the full flavor of my *Sitti's*, my grandmother's, meals. Even if all Sitti could manage to provide for us was bread, she'd stretch her flour and oils and make it perfectly delicious. The gap in the ceiling bugged my father. It bugged me even as a visitor. Every raindrop rolled mockingly down the concrete slab walls, and I knew that this hole was nothing like their home before the occupation.

———

The last time I visited, just one summer ago after my first year of medical school, I noticed some improvements to their home. Just Yabba and I went—"a father and son adventure," he had said, proposing the idea to me. When we arrived, my cousins excitedly greeted me and tugged at my arm, pulling me around the corner to see the flat screen television my dad had shipped a few weeks prior to our departure.

"Look, Jon-a-than!" they shouted.

I smiled and nodded as they flipped the channels, turned it on and off, and used the menu options.

I knew my dad wanted to do more than just make them comfortable, but refugee camp or not, they simply refused to leave the West Bank.

Whenever Yabba tried to persuade them to move to East Jerusalem, the Arab side that is moderately safe, *Sidi*, my grandfather, quickly ended the conversation, shaking his head before my dad could even begin to make his case. "Hasan, we've already been uprooted once, okay?"

———•———

Last summer, I was drinking some Turkish coffee with my cousins and their friend Hideya, who had recently been shot for throwing rocks. As a medical student, I wanted to study the flesh wound in her shoulder and managed to sneak a peak. It was deep and badly mended.

"I wish I had died," she told me. "It would be better to have died." Everyone continued to drink their coffee and chat as normal. It was normal.

"What?" I yelled.

They stopped talking and looked at each other in confusion.

"I threw some rocks because I do not care if I die. I want a life like normal on our old land with the lemon trees." Her eyes were ablaze, blue like flames. "You like the lemons, Jonathan?"

I nodded.

"Our lemons….wow! Wow!" She waved her good arm to gesture the size of the trees.

My cousin Nadia interrupted her movement. "No! No! Our lemon trees were the best!"

I pretended to smile as I listened to them switch to Arabic and bicker about whose lemon trees were better, but the thought of what Hideya said made me really angry.

———•———

In college, some of my American friends told me that I was anti-Semitic. Am I? They told me about God's special relationship with Israel and asked me to please stop calling God "Allah." God and Allah are not the same, Zaytouni, they'd say. I was always all-American Jonathan when I scored a touchdown, but Zaytouni when I was a Palestinian. Want to hear about the Holocaust again? I already knew all about it, but I listened to them anyway. The whole time I couldn't help thinking of my friend Rascal who we invited in our home that dark night.

Guests wear out their welcome, don't they? I realized this as I drove by a settlement in the West Bank during my last visit. It was the largest of all the settlements. *Ma'aleh Adumim*, just east of East Jerusalem. International law forbids such settlements, but no one cares. No one stops it. Instead we get stopped, literally, at all the checkpoints. While we waited at a checkpoint outside of Ma'aleh Adumim, I watched the wall being built around the settlement, extending into Arab Jerusalem and surrounding it, choking it, which has made it even more difficult for my cousins to get to school and my uncle to get to work. Sometimes they just can't make it to class or to work, and Sitti stretches out her flour a little more, a little more. Behind a line of cars at this checkpoint, I studied a Palestinian laborer working on the wall. He never looked up from his work, gripping the rebar and securing the slabs. His forehead was deeply creased with concentration. His brown, wiry body glistened in the merciless afternoon sun. He and the other workers must have toiled away all morning firmly fixing those concrete segments of the wall. I wondered what he might have been thinking. I looked up to the sky and saw a bird flying over the laborers.

"If you cannot beat them, you join them," Yabba told me when he saw the worker from the car window.

Them. The last day of my visit in Israel, I was crowded at a checkpoint, engulfed by a mob of Palestinians wanting to get home at the end of the day. Normally, my dad would handle these situations, but he had left Israel early to speak at a conference in Bahrain. I tried to shove like everyone else did just to stay on our feet. A handicapped man stumbled about as two children teased him, imitating his stagger and mutterings. Everyone was elbowing everyone else. Some women were crying and rocking and fanning their flushed babies in the overheated space. In the middle of the chaos, the man in front of me turned around, looked at my complexion and clothing with disgust, and yelled at me in the little English he must have known.

"Fucking Americans! You do this! You do this!"

I snapped back at him in Arabic, knowing I had a slight American accent. I told him that I was Palestinian, too, like everyone else here, though in that moment, I wasn't proud of it. I could never be proud when I saw my hurt people hurting other people. Sometimes the news flashes about Palestinians are true.

When I finally got up to where the soldiers were, I laughed to find they were eighteen-year-old girls with dark braids and eye makeup thickly painted on like the eye-black that football players wear. They were fulfilling their required military service. Carelessly whirling their M-16s about, they giggled and occasionally returned to seriousness as they inspected us. One of them smiled at me and asked me where I was from in America and let me pass without any more questions. Another scowled, grabbed my arm, and shoved me on. Another said "thank you, have a nice day," proud of her English as she gently handed my American passport back to me.

———•———

The next morning, the sun refused to stay down, so I had to say goodbye to my grandparents and my cousins after only a three week stay. They gave me gifts, little trinkets that they couldn't afford, but in their minds, couldn't afford not to give me—a CD of Arabic music, a blue and white colored ceramic dish, books about the conflict, and a DVD of traditional Arab belly dancers. My grandmother kissed my cheeks multiple times as she cried. I climbed into my rental car. We had rented one with Israeli tags, just to be a little safer.

When my dad had warned me to arrive at the airport three to four hours before my flight, I doubted him. I got to the airport with exactly three hours to spare, and I ended up needing every minute because of the questioning. I showed them my American passport, holding it out with a strong and firm hand, but they just looked at my last name, 'Zaytouni,' which was clearly not a Hebrew name. For hours, five Israeli women interrogated me about why I was visiting family and why I was flying first class if I was only a medical student. Three hours. They rattled me. I'll admit it. I was taken to another room for more questioning. A young man about my age sat behind a shiny, wooden desk, and he smiled. His oversized blazer shifted on his thin shoulders; his crisp collar shimmied up his clean-shaven neck, doused in a strong cologne. He leaned back in the executive chair, rustling the scent that was vaporizing about him.

"What do you call yourself?" he said clearly.

"Jonathan Zaytouni. I'm American."

"Why have you visited?" he asked, his dark eyes looking me in mine.

"I came to visit my family. They live in Bethlehem." I looked around the room and noticed a stethoscope hanging decoratively on the wall. "Are you a doctor?" I asked.

"Soon," he said, glancing at the stethoscope and then returning his attention to me.

"Me, too."

We smiled.

"You can go. Have a safe trip back to America."

———•———

Once on board, I buried my face in the steaming towel that the flight attendant brought me and then leaned my head against the pillow he had supplied without my even asking.

"Something to drink, Mr. Zaytouni?" he asked as he handed me a glossy menu.

"Some scotch. On the rocks."

The plane hummed and taxied on the runway. Tel Aviv Yaffo Airport. I could still feel the energy of my family's soil buried deep beneath layers and layers of concrete on this very spot. I imagined the evacuation at gunpoint in the middle of the night. The demolition of their memories. The lemon trees. The fragrance.

By the time we took off, the scotch was gone. Without any turbulence, the airplane speedily glided above the land, and its tilting wings blended the shared air like a bird.

Screaming

By Nate Leiderbach

He said he had a crossbow, but I don't remember seeing anything, and we didn't turn around after he said not to turn around. I didn't think he had a weapon, and I don't think Brian did either, but we walked off the man's land because even if he didn't impale us he could prosecute, and I'd heard trespass was a felony. We were definitely in the wrong. The barbed fence we'd climbed through was well marked. But there was water in there we'd never fished before, and so it wasn't really a choice. Hiking to the spot where he caught us probably took two miles or more, but we hadn't paid attention, catching so many cuttbow trout, so big for that little nameless stream, we were lost in frenzied ecstasy when the property-owning fuck snuck up. From behind a willow bush, he growled, "Freeze! You're trespassing. *Don't look at me!* I'll plug you both through the spines! I know what you're doing. You're both selfish bastards!"

He told us to step out of the creek and march toward a rocky outcropping. So we marched in the direction he said and past it, and he shouted at us from twenty yards behind. We weren't leaving the way we came in, which was walking the Milsky logging road to his fence and then following its overgrown tracks into heavy forest, balancing over an old rail-tie gulch bridge, scooting down the chalky drop to the smooth-stone bank and then slogging right up the middle of the creek.

"Keep moving, you thieves. No, to the right!" The man wasn't from Colorado. He had a Boston accent and what sounded like too much spit in his mouth. "Keep moving."

So we marched and marched. Brian hummed softly and my adrenaline faded into something robotic. I let the sunlight through the pine and aspen hypnotize me. I thought about many things, dark, tangled things, and watched them slip loose in the light. It was the strangest mood of peace. Everyone I thought of, I thought of in the fondest manner, really, no grudges, and this was a handful of years ago now, in my late twenties, so I'd built quite a few. But at that moment, that single afternoon, my wet boots squeaking out creek water, my nose full of the forest, having no control to begin with, no control to worry about, I forgave all my ex-girlfriends and old college buddies, even my parents. Hell, I forgave some tricky ones too, just to test the water, my sister-in-law for calling the cops on me at her wedding, and my older cousin, dead now from a four-wheeling accident, who'd made me put my dick in his mouth when I was eight.

Keep going, boys. Keep going. And in my healing heart I was walking beside these enemies as a team, marching in protest of life's difficulties, in protest of youth and its lies, its absolutes, its black and whites. Past downy moss trees and through sunlit, wildflower glades, the tip of my fishing pole winking above me and ahead of me like a will-o'-the-wisp, the back of my fishing vest heavy with a full meal of trout, I marched. I could taste the cuttbows, ready to be smoked with lemon and sage over a dancing campfire; I'd share them with these long-lost foes, all our crossbows slack, leaned against trees, everyone laughing real laughs, patting their stomachs, my wife smiling like she did in the beginning…

———•———

Brian stopped, grabbing my arm to make me pull up. Shaking his head, he said, "Shit, I don't even know where we are anymore."

I did some blinking to snap to, looked around, yawned and said nothing. We were on an overgrown logging road, but not the Milsky road, not the one we came in on, down in a depression of earth and rock that was thick with towering cotton-woods.

"I can't even hear the creek," Brian said. "I can't hear the road, can't hear traffic."

I took off my visor, wiped at my hairline sweat. "But he's gone?"

Brian turned around, stepped a few feet, listening, nodding. "Yeah. I don't know when though, maybe ten minutes ago? I was a bit dazed, just walking. Strange, I forgot he was even there."

I put my visor back on. "We didn't go out through his fence. Think he's still watching us?"

Brian didn't reply. He began walking, or strolling, looking up into the tree branches, squinting, maybe trying to position us with the sun, find our way. I followed him, two paces back, wishing I could return to my forgiveness trance, but knowing I never could, like returning to a dream, impossible. Or like a cocaine hangover, yeah, that's how it felt then, a hollowness in my bones, like I knew I was winding up to be much lower than I started. So I kicked a rock. I made it a game, trying to keep it on the road, keep it ten feet ahead of us as we walked, and it hit Brian's heels until he stopped, irritated, not saying anything, giving me a look. He leaned down, snatched the rock and chucked it into the trees. We listened as it snapped off dead branches.

I said, "Bet the dude was deformed. Bet he drooled when he shouted. Probably a hair-lip, some incest baby raised in a mine shaft. Sounded like he was pissed at the world, didn't it? On a power trip."

"Either way," Brian said, "he was in charge."

We hiked five or ten more minutes until Brian slowed and walked in a small circle.

"What?" I said.

He sighed, scratching his cheek. "Damn New Yorker—where the hell are we?"

"That was a Boston accent."

"Fucking tourist."

"Fucking private property," I said. "It's water, it flows onto the property and off it, and the fish don't touch the ground."

"The fish," Brian said quietly to himself, "the fish might spoil. We should have cleaned as we caught."

I took off my vest, dropped my pole, unzipped the long back pocket and removed my catch. The clammy plastic bag was hot. I dumped the three big trout in the middle of the overgrown tire track.

"Christ," Brian said, nodding at me, "here we go with the drama," and as if to argue my actions, he fastened an extra button on his vest and readjusted his own fishes' weight.

"They weren't mine to begin with," I said. "It's all that Boston asshole's fault. The guilt's on him."

Brian gave me his you-idiot look and rolled his eyes, but I was happy I'd gotten some reaction. The last five minutes of hiking had me worried. Brian had been breathing so hard, and walking with no apparent direction, that he didn't seem himself. When we're together, I usually let him take the lead. It's the old marine in him; it's his constant, overwhelming certainty, and it's too much work to argue. What I couldn't figure was, was he merely irritated at being disoriented, or was it guilt that he'd let his guard down, worry that he'd lost trust in his instincts?

He squatted, retied his laces.

"I hope that chicken-shit *is* still watching," I said, and stepped on my fish, squashing them one by one, flesh into dirt, skull and bones crunching. The flies were on it immediately. I said, "The pussy didn't have a crossbow."

"He said he had a gun."

"He said crossbow."

Brian stood. "Jesus, who carries a crossbow? He was from New York, not the Dark Ages."

"Anyway," I said, "I doubt he had a weapon, but I don't need a trespassing suit."

"We got off easy," Brian said. "Know why Killman can't hear in that left ear?"

I counted four flies swarming the meat on my wet right boot.

"You listening to me?"

I wiped the fish guts off in the high bunchgrass. "Who?"

"Killman. Sal's friend. The one whose canoe we borrowed for Morrow Point."

"Oh, yeah."

"Yeah, well he was trespassing right around here, Lincoln Basin, and the property owner, another New Yorker, had him kneel down and told him to say sorry. Said he could just walk away if he said sorry. Killman wouldn't, just cussed the guy. So the property owner fired off a .270 round right next to his head."

"And your point?"

Brian picked up my pole, shoved it at me. "Knock it off. Let's just find the car."

"Boston," I said, "not New York." I crossed my arms, didn't take my pole from him. I said, "Harvard, not Columbia." I put my hands in my pockets, nodded and smiled, rocked on my heels. "Boston Garden, not—"

"Cocksucker," Brian said. He tossed my pole into the woods and started walking. The guy's got three inches on me and lanky strong. I never win. But I went for him anyway, my arm around his neck, throwing myself, feet out. I whipped him right off his feet, and he landed four rabbit punches to my right kidney as we fell. He's not a touchy one, either, doesn't even like shaking hands, and he's always bitching about personal space, bubbles, stay out of my bubble, back off, man, *I'm warning you.*

Shit, I was laughing, just cranking down on his neck, elbow still locked, ass on the dirt, Brian's body trailing behind me, his left fist working my kidney and spine and thigh. We stank, fish flesh and sweat and breakfast breath, but we were young and strong. Huffing and never laughing himself, all business, Brian patiently bruised my side, punch by punch, until someone screamed.

We froze. It wasn't me and it wasn't him. Even our heavy panting caught.

After a beat, I inhaled slowly. I let Brian work his head free. He stood, shook out his legs, cocked his head to hear. I stood up too, trying to stay quiet, listening. After a minute of silence, I whispered, "The hair-lip's fucking with us."

Brian frowned, shook his head. After another minute without a sound, I shrugged and he shrugged, then he cracked the flat of his palm into my solar plexus, knocked the wind right out of me and grinned. My eyes bulged and I staggered backwards, fighting to keep my feet. Regaining my breath, I held onto a tree and that's when we heard the scream again. It was a woman. But it was only part scream, mostly moan. Instantly, Brian was off, swiping up his pole then tiptoe-jogging through the woods, with me, after finding my rod, on his heels.

•————•

We hunkered behind a boulder, peering around its ragged side. The woman was clutching a tree trunk, back bent, arms straight, head down. Her pants were down too. She had blond hair and it trembled as the man behind her, hands on her waist, his pants dropped and his white ass clenched, pumped. He gripped her hips with just his fingertips, digging, kneading. She tossed her hair but we couldn't see her face. She screamed again, not pleasant or real at all, and barked, "You can go harder!"

The man paused, rolled his head, massaged his side. A cramp. He was old, fifties, I'd guess. We couldn't see his face, either, but he had moles all over his back and patches of brown hair. He slapped at his shoulder blade like going for a mosquito, and got back to thrusting.

"You think," the woman huffed—and we could hear her clearly; they weren't more than twenty feet away, "you can come?" She readjusted her hands on the trunk, arching her lower back, a diamond wedding ring flashing in the sun.

The man didn't answer, but stomped his foot.

"It's okay if you can't," the woman said. "I know I can't."

After a twenty second delay of just pumping, the man spoke. His voice was high-pitched and electronic sounding. He said, "Scream again."

The woman lifted her head, though we still couldn't see her face, and screamed. She said, "Like that?"

"Good."

She screamed again and shook her hips side to side. The man's butt cheeks clenched. He had zits on his ass, and I remember all I could think at first was, absurdly, Hey, I bet they've been driving a lot through some hot country.

She screamed again, two short bursts.

He said, "Good. Good." He stomped his right foot, stomped his left, snorted like a bull. "Good." But he yanked away. Pants on his ankles, he hopped to the side and just started pissing, bending into it, butt cheeks really clenching now. "Good," that strange voice hummed, "good," and I listened to the urine splatter against the leaves, sporadic but hard. Then, crouching, but still pissing, he wrenched up his pants, secured his belt, and hurried off. Fifteen feet away, he turned once, all the way around, and looked at the woman but she didn't look at him, didn't move from her position. He had a long, fresh scar from his throat to almost his belly button, dot scars running along each side. The crotch of his jeans was piss-soaked, his face emotionless.

We watched him go, disappearing into the trees, but the woman stayed as she was, not moving except for squeezing the aspen trunk. She sighed, protracted, exhausted. I looked at Brian. His face was bloodless, eyes half closed. And then he glared at me. I looked back at the woman, at the dark seam of her crotch, trying to make out something, the rich brown ring of her anus, or a glint of moisture on her silhouetted tangle of pubes. Nothing but a dark seam. I thought, *That could just as well be Kate.* I was still married then. Kate and I hadn't yet cheated on each other. We still held each other after sex. We still kissed sometimes during orgasm. But she didn't fish and she didn't like to talk, and if I ever slept in on a morning she wanted us to get housework done, she banged and slammed things. But those were the little things. Mostly she just hated fishing. When we first met, she loved that I fished, and that was enough. But then she wanted to be a part of each second of my life. I took her, but it bored her to no end. I even showed her my favorite spot at Miner Cove, loaded with browns that looked like they could swallow muskrats, and she started throwing rocks in the water. So I threw a rock *near* her—we didn't speak for two days.

The woman holding the tree muttered something unintelligible.

Brian ground his teeth. How he looked at that moment is stained on my brain. Sometimes I have a hard time envisioning people's faces, even people close to me, people I see every day. I can get a lock on one or two of their features, the thickness of an eyebrow, the curve of a cheekbone, but the harder I try, the more distorted and ghastly their faces appear. Crouched behind that boulder, I'd never seen Brian so pale, so disconcerted, eyelids drooping. Was it the intimacy, the gross biology, the fact that we couldn't walk away? Maybe, but I wasn't concerned with his thoughts; I was suddenly lost in the idea that he might faint. I'd never seen him collapse, weakened, and the thought thrilled me. I'd take care of him, prop his feet up for treatment of shock, rest a damp cloth on his face.

The woman shook her head, the blond hair waving, and tried the scream again, over and over, changing the pitch up to down. She moved her right hand to her crotch like she knew we were focused on it, and screamed again.

Then she straightened up, back still to us, her thighs dimpled, but her hair long and luscious on the small of her back. She pulled her shirt off her shoulders and down, pulled up her skirt—it wasn't pants—and walked in the direction the man had walked. When she was twenty-five yards off, I started after her, but Brian grabbed my vest. I spun around and smacked him, open handed, on the side of the head, his ear, and then I hopped out of reach. I don't know if he followed me then or when. I don't know if he saw what I did. One second I was alone in the campground parking lot and the next he was beside me.

Josie, my girlfriend now, she likes to fish, loves to. That's when we get along best. She works one bank, I work the other, but she won't trespass or fish without a license. Our first date was two days after Kate and I finalized our divorce. It was a warm October Sunday. I didn't tell Josie she was using Kate's pole and wearing Kate's fishing vest, and she never asked. We drove out to the reservoir and jigged Truss Cove. Josie had landed one small brown, which I showed her how to release with minimal trauma, and was working the hook out of a second when a game warden strolled up. He had a kind, boyish face and held himself in a manner that seemed he wasn't quite comfortable with confrontation. Neither Josie nor I had licenses. I'd promised her we were fine, it was Sunday, middle of hunting season, and we wouldn't be bothered. "Plus," I had added, "we're not keeping anything. And if you look at it this way, none of the fish we'll catch are even native to Colorado, and the reservoir isn't supposed to even exist—"

She laughed. "Interesting."

"—and it's our taxes that pay for the stocking, for the hatchery—"

"Okay. Relax," she smiled. "You trying to convince me or yourself?"

The game warden watched Josie release her second brown, and good-naturedly applauded her catch and release skills. Then he asked if I'd caught anything. I said no, and we joked about Josie's beginner's luck and getting skunked by your woman, and then he said sorry to bother us but it's his job to peek our licenses. Coolly, I pretended to reach for my wallet that wasn't there. I patted my back pocket and frowned.

"Is it in your truck?" the warden said.

"No," I said, "in my wallet and ... that's right, I completely left it—"

Josie nodded her head. "You did." She said, "Baby, I told you to grab it off the breakfast bar."

"Well," he said, "it happens."

Josie held something out for him, a little card, maybe her diver's license, saying, "Here you go."

The man smiled at it and nodded. "Perfect. You're good to go. Thank you very much, Kate." He handed it back to her, and turned to me. "Don't worry, happens all the time. I'll just scratch you up a ticket and you get your license down to our office within a couple weeks, and we'll tear her up. Get back to fishing. Looks like you've got some catching up to do."

I thanked him and shook his hand. Before he shuffled off, he tipped the brim of his hat at Josie, grinned and said, "Don't catch too many more fish than him. A good wife knows when her hubby's self-confidence is on the line."

We didn't fish anymore, but drove the truck up Truss Gulch. Why did Kate keep a current license in her vest if she hated fishing? Was she hoping she'd learn to like it?

This thought bothered me, but I had to let it go and focus on the narrow four-wheel road. There were hunters everywhere you looked, fat and bleary eyed, their massive bellies trembling against the handlebars of their ATVs. We past countless tent sites but only counted two trucks with Colorado plates; everybody else was from Texas, Oklahoma, Nebraska, and New Jersey. Josie said, "God, look at all this litter. Plastic bags, beer cans, shot-up coolers—disgusting."

I said, "That fucking Boy Scout warden needs to grow some balls and write tickets up here."

Josie shook her head. It was starting to sprinkle. "At least he wasn't a dick."

"He wrote me a ticket."

She smiled, shook her head again, looked out her window.

"What?"

"Nothing."

"Come on."

She sighed. "For a second there, watching you lie to the guy, I thought I *was* Kate."

"Don't worry. You don't know Kate. You're not."

"Good," she said, "because I didn't like you very much."

———•———

I abandoned Brian and trailed the woman when she left the tree, watching my steps, watching for brittle twigs, and under my breath saying, "Keep going. Keep going." I don't know if I was talking to myself or her, but I walked, halted, cautious, ready to duck behind a stump or boulder, and I felt all my old grudges returning and I welcomed them. I felt powerful. We would find Brian's car, find the house of the Boston rancher, and damage something of his. Break windows, tear down a fence, cut the throats out of his sheep and drape them over his marital headboard.

Thirty yards ahead of me, the woman clawed her way up an embankment, batting her arms through the low branches of a row of pines, and beyond her I made out the silver of a vehicle. For a brief moment, a bright flash of anger hit my brain, my muscles locked, and I bared my teeth. Who were this man and woman to do their disgusting fetish fucking in the serenity of my forests, in my backyard? Why did I have to see that?

I circled around the embankment, staying low around a Forest Service outhouse, maneuvering my fishing pole through the fir scrub, and stepped out into the dirt lot on its far side, across from the woman and man. They had the van's sliding door open, and, reaching into the backseat, the woman gathered a sleeping child and handed it to the husband. Then she gathered a second one for herself, and they stood side by side cooing and rocking the babies. I noticed the man had changed out of his piss-pants and into shorts. He waved. I waved back. I sat down on a parking space rail tie, set down my rod, and fished a bent Swisher Sweet from my vest. In my pants pocket, I found a lighter. I puffed and watched the babies rocked. From what I could see, the man had a round face with little, lost features, but he smiled and smiled. The woman didn't. She was all business, rocking her baby with a distinct, curt rhythm.

The couple put the babies back in the minivan, secured them in their car seats, and closed the door. That's when I stood and strolled over.

The man had climbed in the passenger side, his door still open, tugging at his seatbelt. The woman adjusted the driver's seat and rolled down her window. I stopped about ten feet off and the man looked up, saying in that electronic voice, "Catch anything?"

I nodded.

He nodded and smiled. He wasn't as old as I thought, late thirties, tops, just weathered, his features tiny, scrunched together like they could fit on a tea saucer. His head though, it was massive, surreal. Politely, he rolled down his window before closing his door. He looked at the sky, played with his neck. "Well, good to hear. And it's a gorgeous day."

The woman looked around the parking lot, bending over the wheel, frowning through the windshield, her nose sharp and long, her mouth tight, her eyes a gray-blue. When she turned to me, turned those eyes, it felt the opposite I thought it would; she owned me. Her lips moved. "Where's your car?"

I said, "You got me," and then I forced a laughed.

The man laughed too, and then nodded and said, "You lost, Chief?"

I couldn't think of what to say then. I shook my head, and in their faces I could see he was worried for me, and she was worried for no one. Chief? Here was a man who had his chest pried open, god knows what they took out or put in. Chief, huh? They weren't worried for themselves, not at all. Why not? What if I had a knife, a gun? What if I wanted to kidnap their children?

"Okay," the woman said.

"Hope you find your car," the man said.

I nodded, took a drag. Blowing it out, I said, "Pretty confident I will." I looked through the back windows of their van. The kids were asleep. Out cold. Babies. Twins maybe? That's what all the rebound girls asked, like an after thought, always after sex, always in the morning when I couldn't bare to look at them. Cheeks to the pillow, tickling my bare chest with perfect nails, they'd stare at my profile and ask, "You didn't … did you and Kate have any kids?"

I'd say, "Butler. Thirteen." Their nails would halt, dig. You could almost hear their hearts drying out.

"Is…is he okay with the divorce?"

"As long as Kate remembers to change his litter. Kids, no, we never tried."

They'd giggle—the nails moving again, the hearts reinflating, inhaling relief. But Josie and I have been together over two years and she's never asked, and the more I think about it, that's a problem, isn't it?

The woman turned the minivan over and said, "Have a nice afternoon."

Nodding to the backseat, the man flashed me a look that said he was sorry his wife was brusque, then began rolling up his window. "A.C.," he said, "for the kids."

I nodded, took another long drag, and listened to the van slip easily into drive. They pulled slowly away. The van had a bike rack on the back, but no bikes. The plates were South Dakota, and a bumper sticker read, "I'D RATHER BE HERE NOW."

———•———

I first had sex with Josie that Sunday evening after the game warden caught us. I'd had a string of rebound one-night stands during my separation with Kate, but those girls, gorgeous when we crawled into bed, all looked monstrous in the morning light. I didn't want that to happen with Josie. Rain slapped against our window. I couldn't get a hard-on. We were napping, our skin still sage-coated, rain in our hair, and she touched my belly and I shivered. I got up, pretended I was thirsty, pretended I had a foot cramp, pretended I … well, I ran out of things to pretend and finally just sat next to her on the bed and said, "I'm sorry. I'm not good at mixing sex and friendship. And I can't get hard because I like you so much."

She said, "I'm flattered." She smiled, so real, and kissed my bare back. Kissed it four times. It worked. We had sex. Fast. Perfect. And then we slept, just our feet touching, fast, perfect.

Josie—I can feel her leaving already, leaving because I'm too confident pretending I'm someone I'm not. Someday … someday, just like I miss Kate, I'll miss her too. But can anyone give me another option, another way to protect what's mine?

———•———

From under my visor, I watched the man and woman pull to a stop at the parking lot exit. Highway 26. I knew where Brian and I were then, and it was a strange bit of disappointment that we'd never been as lost as we'd thought.

The minivan's left blinker clicked on. The brake lights snapped off with a purr of engine. Was it a gorgeous day? Would it sound less creepy if I said it was raining? If I said their van was rusted and the windows poorly tinted? If a mangled tricycle dangled from the bike rack?

As the woman pulled onto the highway, I took the cigar from my mouth and screamed.

The van jerked to a halt.

I screamed again, changing my pitch, feeling my lungs work perfectly, my heart pump, my chest muscles tighten, my stale breath banging against my teeth. I screamed and screamed, contorting my face, flailing my tongue, waving my arms, and they sped away.

———•———

Of course I didn't have a fishing license, but I wasn't gonna look that Boy Scout in the face and debate my stance on federal wildlife management. Sure he was pleasant, but also an idiot, doing his job all wrong, walking the reservoir banks because he was too terrified to confront the hunters in the outlying timber.

At home, I followed the directions on my ticket, wrote out the check for fifty bucks, and mailed it in. Two weeks later I got a letter from the warden. Upon discovering I'd lied to him, that I hadn't had a license in years, he fined me another fifty dollars. Where he signed the letter, in big, junior-high cursive, he wrote: *I thought you were a really nice couple. Now I've lost some hope in people.*

But that's not all that was in the envelope. There was a fifty dollar ticket fine for Kate since Josie used her license.

"I'm shoving this in her mailbox!" I said. "She won't have a clue."

"Give me that," Josie said, ripping it from my hands.

———•———

From the parking lot, it was a four-mile walk back to Brian's car. We tried to hitch, but no one would stop. The entire way, Brian didn't say a word. His face was still pale, arms flopping by his sides. Once, I whistled, and he glared at me. At his car, he told me to take off my boots, put them in the back; the fish guts stunk and he couldn't take it. After that, he ignored me, just flipped on music and we drove with the windows down. When he dropped me off at home, he said, "You or Kate want my fish?"

"Naw."

"I'm just going to throw them away. I feel guilty, but Jesus…"

"You alright?"

He shook his head, played with the rearview mirror. "No," he answered, not looking at me. "No."

I stepped from the car, leaned in the open door. I was fine. I was happy. I was happy with my decision not to speak with my parents for another year. Happy I hated my dead cousin and my sister-in-law. "Me neither," I said, but I didn't mean it.

Brian said, "That was the saddest thing I ever saw, but what bothers me is that I don't know why…."

As his voice trailed off, I nodded. I was already changing the story for Kate, already whittling down the emotion, inflating the horrific parts. I smiled at Brian, "What was, Chief? The chicken-shit with the crossbow?"

Brian gunned it, drove off, the car door yanked from my hand.

———•———

At this moment, Josie and I are driving home from fishing Miner's Cove all afternoon. Her voice has wrenched me from my quiet recollections, the hypnotic yellow lines of the highway. She's talking firmly, defensively, coming clean that she took Kate's fishing fine, paid it, and also wrote the warden a reply. She claims her letter was merely an earnest apology for being a follower rather than an ethical leader. I sigh, squeeze the steering wheel. I tell her it isn't about that; I tell her it's simply about whose side she's on.

"That," she says, "is none of your business."

I pull onto the highway shoulder, my foot hard on the brake.

"Pretty much," she says, "I simply asked the warden not to lose hope in people."

Shaking my head, I bend over the steering wheel and calmly say, "No, Josie, it isn't any of my business. Just like it wasn't your business to fucking apologize for me."

She turns her shoulder, just clams up. Typical. I smack on the left turn signal and swerve onto the highway. I just want to get home, get some space from this woman, permanent space, but around the next bend is a goddamn station wagon on some fucking Sunday drive. They're easily ten miles under the speed limit, so I flash my lights, but they won't let me pass. I can see Josie in my periphery, red-faced, clutching her seatbelt with both hands. I ride the station wagon's ass, my lights on and off in their tinted back window, but they don't budge, don't change their speed for two miles, never reach out the window and give me the finger.

Know what? I'm impressed. Outside of town, I back off, give them a good forty feet. They spray their wiper fluid. The mist arcs over their roof, high and radiant into the leveling sun, before softly splattering my windshield.

"Apologize for *you*?" Josie says. "Can *you* apologize for *me*?"

Turning onto our street, I reach for my wiper lever. I reach, but all I know is by the time I've pulled it down, we're already in the driveway, the key out of the ignition.

Miss Lorena's Nightshirt

By Laurie Wagner Buyer

1.

Not knowing Jesse's last name did not trouble Lorena at all. Not knowing where he went or when he would come back bothered her more than she cared to admit. Her life ran that way. Things that were important to others did not matter to her. But other things, often small, seemingly insignificant things, mattered a great deal. Like now, sitting in the sun on the riverbank, her skin wet and open to the air, she wondered if anyone else noticed the things she did, like the way the breeze ruffled the ungrazed grass so that the September seed heads shivered, dancing together. The last dance of summer now that everything had gone gold.

She checked Jesse's shirt where it was draped, freshly washed, over the half-leafed branches of a waist high willow. Nearly dry. She straightened the thin upright collar, pulled the sleeves and cuffs, pressed the multiple handcrafted pleats and tucks between her palms. A dull, rust colored stain ran from the waistline to the hem on the left side of the once white Swiss cotton shirt that now bordered on ivory gray. Touching each of seven small, polished antler buttons, she knew the shirt had been lovingly made by someone who knew her stitches.

Far off, the town's church bells rang. Lorena dressed slowly, taking time to make certain her pantaloons and petticoats were smooth, her gingham dress not crumpled. She tucked her damp hair up under her bonnet, rolled Jesse's shirt and secured it at her waist under her skirt. The line-backed dun she borrowed from the livery nickered at her approach, and Lorena stroked his neck, murmuring love words, saying his name, "Whiskey, Whiskey." She missed the spunky gray mare she used to ride before Jesse came, but Whiskey was sweet-tempered and she treasured his company. Untying the reins from an aspen sapling, she shinnied up on the gelding and rode back to town.

The streets of Melville were dusty despite yesterday's afternoon rain. At the livery, Hobbes tipped his hat as he took the horse.

"Morning, Miss Lorena."

"Morning, Mr. Hobbes."

"Lovely day," he commented.

"Yes, it is."

"Thank you for letting me borrow Whiskey."

"Anytime, Miss Lorena, anytime."

Her back straight, her steps measured and even, her eyes modestly down, she walked toward the center of town. When she met others on the boardwalk, she moved to the side and waited for them to pass. Women muttered words out the sides of their mouths. Men glanced, stiff and silent. Unknowing young girls eyed her. Boys, shoving and giggling, pointed. The names they called out flapped around her like crows. In her first year at Melville House, the pain and humiliation had nearly killed her, kept her huddled up in her room until she shriveled in its airless, sunless confines. Only Miss Mabel's motherly attention had saved her.

"There now, Rina," Miss Mabel had soothed. "You ain't got no cause to cry. There ain't no shame in loving men. Ain't your fault God ended you up here. Get on out of the house now and walk. Go on down to the river."

So Lorena walked miles every day at dawn when the weather allowed, and on Sundays she often borrowed a horse to ride. She learned the names of plants, like the sweet-smelling heart-leaf bitter cress which grew at the water's edge, and the minute, fragile-flowered fairy candelabra. Passing seasons eased her loss and she took solace in the beaver that built their house near her favorite swimming spot. She gave up trying to attend church and set Sundays aside to worship the gods who lived at the river. She heard their voices in the wind, in the river's rush over rocks, in the rustle of grass and leaves, or the breathy snort of does who came to drink with their fawns. The deep pool was cool and felt like dark silk against her skin. Swimming was as close as she came to praying anymore.

2.

Returning to her room at Melville House, which ordinary folks called Mabel's Place, Lorena straightened her bed and settled in a chair by the window to handwork a piece of embroidery. A calico kitten that Hobbes had given her played with the strands of colored thread dangling near her feet. Sometimes it seemed that Jesse was nothing but a dream, yet she remembered everything with such clarity. She had been at her dresser the night he came, twisting up her hair when she heard movement at her open door.

"Be with you in a minute, Scottie," she had said. When there was no answer she turned and saw a tired looking stranger leaning against the door frame. He nodded, the barest movement of his head, then stepped in and closed the door.

"Scottie's not coming," he said.

His gravel-rough voice made her pause. He was not handsome. Large, dirty, worn looking, he had cautious, flat, green-brown eyes and long, nearly white hair that brushed the collar of his faded buckskin coat. His face was shadowed with a dusty gray beard. He moved stiffly across the room, favoring his left leg, and Lorena noticed a long rip across the hip of his trousers. He tossed his coat on a straight-backed chair.

"Call me Jesse, Lorena,"

"How'd you know my name?" she asked.

"Mabel told me. I asked her for someone quiet," he answered.

"But, Scottie—"

"Quit worrying about Scottie. Mabel will take care of him. I paid her enough to do it and keep her mouth shut."

In the mirror Lorena watched him sit on the edge of the bed and eye her reflection: a small woman standing primly in a blue cotton wrapper, her feet bare, a hairbrush in hand. She wore no paint and had the face of a woman who didn't mind the sun. An annoyed look flashed in her dark chocolate eyes.

He hung his spurs on the bedpost, pulled off his boots, dropped them on the bare wood floor, then stretched out. Positioning the poor excuse of a pillow, he tipped his hat forward, settling his hips and shoulders with a pleasured groan.

"Come here," he said.

"I don't think—" she began.

"You don't think Mabel would allow some poor, beaten, broke down, no good, thieving son-of-a-bitch like me in her place? Well, I've known Mabel since she was knee-high, and besides, she owes me. Now come here."

Lorena plunked her brush on the dresser, stepped over to the bed and began untying her wrapper.

"Just leave it on," Jesse grumbled from under his hat. He held out his right arm to her as he massaged his left hip with his other hand.

Lorena circled the bed and sat on its edge. He touched her back, letting his hand stay palm flat against her spine. She knew he felt the fear in her. He tugged at her shoulder until she lay down next to him, her body rigid. He waited and when Lorena did not move or speak he muttered, "Goddamn it woman! You could at least act like you like me."

"Well, I don't!" she snapped.

"You're about as talkative and friendly as a snake," he said.

"Didn't you say you wanted someone quiet?"

Jesse grunted. He slipped off his hat and placed it on the bedpost. Leaning over he pulled the pins from Lorena's hair and spread the loosened strands down around her shoulders.

"Your hair's the color of honey," he said. Shifting his shoulders into the thin mattress, he pulled her to his side. Soon, his breathing evened out and he slept.

Lorena watched night rob the last iridescent light from the window. A flimsy spring breeze blew the muslin curtain in and out below the raised glass. She could smell the musk of manure and urine from the street below, and a whiff of budding cottonwoods blown up from the river. Sounds of the saloon slunk under the door: Somebody banging away at a piano. Chairs scraping the floor. Loud voices. Laughter. A string of low-pitched profanity. Mabel's ringing chatter. The occasional sound of boots and high heels on the stairs or along the hallway. The opening and closing of doors.

She breathed in Jesse's ripe odor: old sweat, new sweat, horse sweat, dried blood, unwashed hair, wood smoke, and some piney, mint-like hint she could not place. She moved to get up, but Jesse rolled and stretched his leg over hers.

"Stay," he said.

Hours ticked by. The noise of night revelers softened, but did not cease. Lorena slept.

She woke to the sound of spurs crossing the floor and a watery whoosh as Jesse relieved himself in the chamber pot. Having his boots on meant he was leaving. He moved to the window and she saw him outlined in the dim starlight. He looked out a long while, then closed the casement, paced to the door, then back to the bed. Feeling for the folded quilt at the bottom of the mattress, he shook it open and floated it across Lorena's legs, then drew the edge up over her shoulders.

A commotion on the stairs sent him scurrying, scooping up his hat and coat as he flattened himself against the wall behind the door. Lorena lay unmoving on her side. The door burst open and a gold bar of lamplight spilled inside.

"Lorena?" a man's voice boomed. "Earl Flint. You alone in there?"

"I told you she was alone," Mabel said. "She's been sick. Leave her be."

"Lorena?"

"Yes, Sheriff."

"You alone."

"Yes."

"Seen anyone tonight?"

Knowing she'd reveal her wrapper and unbound hair, she sat up. The lamp's glow would show her frail and pale. She heard Jesse's light intake of air.

"No," she said. "I've been sick."

"Damn!" Flint swore and spun away. "Check the other rooms," he ordered. "Mabel I know you're lying to me. You cater to that renegade."

Their voices faded down the hall.

Jesse shrugged on his coat, then returned to the bed, hat in hand.

"Can you help me?" he asked.

"I can try," she said.

The door opened a crack.

"Jesse?" Mabel whispered. "He's gone. Hobbes swore he saw you riding south toward Point Butte. You're lucky. Lorena's Flint's favorite. He rousted everyone else out."

"I owe you Mabel," Jesse said.

"About time," she said. "I'll give Lorena your things. She can meet you at the river."

The door closed. Lorena's heart skittered in the silent aftermath of surprise and fear.

"Can you meet me then?" he asked.

"When?"

"In an hour or so when Mabel gives you my stuff," he said.

"Yes."

"I'll need a horse."

Lorena thought of Hobbes' gray mare.

"There's one at the livery I borrow. A mare. She's small."

"That'll do, "Jesse said. "Don't bother with a saddle. Just bridle her."

He ruffled her hair like she was his kid sister, then he pushed up off the bed and opened the window with caution. Below, a cluster of cowboys from one of the ranches in the valley rounded the corner. They exchanged goodnights, laughing, mounted up and rode off. Jesse looked back at Lorena sitting on the bed, the quilt wrapped around her like a stole. He nodded, sat on the sill, then was gone. She heard him hit the ground, the muffled grunt of pain as his bad leg collapsed, and the light, quick singing of his spurs as he limped away.

———•———

She moved to the chair, tucked her legs under her wrapper and snuggled into the quilt. How strange the night had been. How strange her life. Her parents and younger brother sick and their wagon left behind as the train wound on to the west. The long hours she tended and nursed and kept the fire going and carried water and picked out rocky pits for their graves. The nothingness that settled over her like a gray pall and she wondered why she lived when they all died. Then the last of the meal and flour running out and she knew of nothing to do but stay by the wagon to keep coyotes from digging up her family. The horses wandered off and Lorena, at seventeen, weak with loneliness and hunger and fear did not care. A scout from a following train passed by, loaded her on his horse like a sack of grain, and dumped her off at the mining town of Melville two days later.

She had no family. No kin to write to even if she had known her letters. No one cared except Mabel and the other girls. And Hobbes, with his crippled stump of an arm, who understood about being outcast and alone.

She hated the men at first. She was slow to learn, but in two years she figured out how to spot the bad ones, the ones who crawled through the door, their eyes small and hard. They were quick and cruel and she knew they beat their wives, so she learned to shut her eyes and close her soul to them.

Some, like the boys just in off the trail, were so awkward and uncertain that she wrapped them in smiles and easy laughter, untied their tongues and taught them the art of talk and touch, took them over the line into the men they'd be someday.

With time she began to wait and long for those men who handled horses for a living; their eyes so open she could see entire landscapes in them, places she had never been except in dreams. Their hands, callused and slow, soothed her, moved like magic over her skin until her nostrils flared and she reared to meet their sound and smell. For days afterward they stayed on her tongue, echoed in her ears.

Jesse. He had barely touched her except to loosen her hair. Who was he? Why was Flint after him?

———

Mabel opened the door.

"You've got to get down to the river and take Jesse his things. Go the back way. Stay in the shadows. You can do it, can't you? If I go, Flint will have his hounds on me."

"I can do it. Mabel, who is. . ."

"Don't ask, girl. Just get dressed and go."

Lorena switched the roll of clothes to her other shoulder and crossed the street toward the stable. Leaving the awkward bundle by a cottonwood near the stock tank, she walked over to the corral. The horses shuffled and blew. In the rising moonlight she could make out their moving shapes. She whispered, "Daisy…Daisy" and puckered her lips with the sound the mare herself made. When a gray shape drifted ghost-like out of the herd, Lorena felt along the barn wall for a bridle. The mare came to her, making soft sounds, nuzzling her open hand.

Standing on the edge of the trough, Lorena balanced Jesse's things on the mare's back, then bunched up her skirt and petticoats and slid on. She trotted away from the sleeping town, reached the dark cover of pines, followed the wagon road until she gained the river. Easing along its edge, working her way around willow clumps, she paused often to listen.

"Here," Jesse said, emerging from the shadows. He grabbed the bundle and scooped Lorena off the mare's back. He ran his hands down the mare's legs to check for soundness and shoes.

"She'll do," he said.

He spread the bundle on the ground sorting out shirt, pants, socks, and bandanas. He picked up a small round object and held it to his nose.

"Only Mabel," he said, smiling.

In the pale light he stripped off his filthy clothes and, taking the soap, he stepped into the chilly water, gasping. Lorena stood by Daisy's head as he washed and splash-rinsed.

When he crawled up the grassy bank, he was laughing. It was a dulcet sound.

"Lord Almighty! That water's come right off a glacier." He shook his head, and droplets flew from his hair and beard disappearing like fallen stars into the grass.

Jesse dried himself with his old shirt, and it soaked up a seep of blood from his reopened wound. He spread his coat on the ground and held out his hand to Lorena. She could have said no, could have walked away, yet he intrigued her, sparked a flicker of desire in the small of her back. Curiosity urged her into taking his hand.

Seeming anxious and somewhat unsteady, he undressed her, but with the first feel of his hands along her hips she knew there was no cruelty in him. She tasted desperation in his mouth, though he did not hurry, kissing her, touching her neck and shoulders. She felt him pacing himself to her breathing. A scattered chorus of frogs tuned up, built their song to a crescendo, quieted, then began again.

●————●

"I shouldn't stay much longer," he said. Taking a small can from his coat pocket, he scooped out a finger full of salve and smeared it on the gash across his hip. The tarry stuff was pungent with herbs and pine. He dressed quickly, then helped Lorena, fumbling over her buttons, running his fingers through her hair. He murmured sweet words that pealed off his tongue like the echo of far-away church bells. He said "Lorena" over and over again until she smiled at the sound of her own name. He pulled her close, then waltzed her swiftly around in the grass until they laughed together, breathless.

"What's that song you're humming?" she asked.

"Don't you know it? You should. It's your name. Lorena."

"No, I've never heard it before. Where is it from?"

"From the war. The men used to sing it around the fires at night."

"Sing it for me, Jesse. Will you?"

He spun her around once more and pressed her back into his chest, held her hands at her waist, and swayed with her, his lips close to her ear as he sang in a throaty off-key tenor:

> The years creep slowly by, Lorena
> The snow is on the grass again
> The sun's low down the sky, Lorena
> The frost gleams where the flowers have been
> But the heart throbs on as warmly now
> As when summer days were nigh
> Oh, the sun can never dip so low
> A-down affection's cloudless sky.

"Oh, it's lovely. A love song, right?"

"Yes. Lovers separated by the war."

She tried to turn and kiss him, but he patted her shoulder and placed her away from his side.

Retrieving his gun belt, he snugged it over his hips and checked the Colt's action. He kicked his old clothes aside and wrapped the hardtack and jerky in the cotton bandana.

"Bury those clothes, okay?" Jesse said as he untied the mare.

"You'll be back?" she asked.

"Of course," he said.

"Jesse," she said, turning his name into a prayer, "be careful."

"I will."

Though she rose up on tiptoes to reach his lips, he did not kiss her again. Instead, he held her face, brushed his thumbs over her glistening eyelashes.

He turned away, grabbed a handful of the mare's mane and leapt astride, grunting at the pain in his hip. Lorena struggled not to cry as he gigged the mare into a jog.

"Her name's Daisy," she said to the night.

———•———

When the sky brightened and the sun poked a smoky red halo over the horizon, Lorena was still at the river. She gathered up Jesse's dirty clothes and ducked into the thick willows looking until she found a hollow under an exposed root. With her hands she dug out dried leaves and debris to make a bigger hole, then stuffed in the torn pants, socks and bandana. Her hands lingered a moment on Jesse's bloodstained shirt. She folded it, tucked it under her skirt, took one last look at the riverbank, then began the walk back to town.

Earl Flint met her halfway. Mounted on a racy, stocking-legged sorrel, he looked down at her, touching his hat.

"Hobbes' gray mare is missing," he said by way of greeting. "Know anything about it?"

"I borrowed her, Sheriff. Something spooked her by the sand bars downriver and she spilled me. I imagine she'll be along in a while."

"Thought you were sick, Lorena."

"I was, Sheriff. I'm feeling much improved since my ride."

"Isn't dawn a bit early to be out riding?"

"Not for me," she said.

Flint studied her flushed face, her hastily wound hair, the absence of a bonnet. He tipped his hat and said, "Watch yourself, Lorena."

"I will, Sheriff. Thank you."

3.

That night, after the town's miners and the boys from the Box R left, she turned out her lamp and washed at the basin, pouring tepid water from a large pitcher. She took Jesse's shirt out from under the mattress and put it on, shivering. She rolled up the too-long sleeves and fastened the hand-cut buttons. The hem hung nearly to her knees. In bed, she hugged herself and let Jesse's wild scent comfort her.

Saturday night of that same week welded itself in her brain, for that was the beginning of Clancy Melville's visits to her room. The minute she had to face his slit-like eyes and small pink hands close up, she hated him and his fine cut clothes, the smell of his hair oil and stout cologne. Polite-talking and smooth-gestured, he nonetheless made her skin crawl. Lorena had seen him in the saloon with petite, dark-haired Sophie, but she had also seen him and his tight-lipped wife on the streets. That Saturday night he was pompous and rough. When he was gone, Lorena scrubbed herself raw and cried, and clutched the front of Jesse's shirt until she slept.

The next morning at the river she washed the shirt for the first time and swam away her simmering anger. When she returned, she confronted Mabel in the back yard.

"How could you send Melville to me?" she asked.

"I didn't send him, Sugar, he asked for you now that Sophie's run off with that big-mouthed Baxter boy out at the Box R."

"Well, don't let him come to me again!" Lorena said.

"Excuse me? As if I could do that when Hobbes and Flint and Scottie all come to you!"

"Mabel, please," Lorena cried, "Melville's mean."

"I can't help that. In case you've forgotten, he's the reason we all eat around here. What's gotten into you anyway?"

Lorena toyed with the fringes on her summer shawl.

Mabel snorted. "Good God, child. Get over it. He's gone."

"He said he'd come back."

"Well, if you believe that then you're way dumber than I figured you to be. Jesse ain't never stuck nowhere for no one."

"Oh, Mabel, what'll I do?"

The older woman gathered Lorena to her ample bosom and rocked her. "You just go on. That's all. It won't hurt forever. It never does."

4.

Summer drifted by, hot and humid. Afternoon storms lightened the air and greened up the grass. Lorena's life revolved around the Saturday night episodes with Clancy Melville. He bought her fancy gifts: satin and lace wrappers, heeled shoes, bonnets with ribbons and bows, earbobs and perfume. When he caught Lorena dressed in her plain cotton gown, barefoot, and unpainted, it infuriated him. Still, she refused to chat or primp or preen for him like Sophie had.

September eased into October, cooling the nights of the Indian summer days. The first Sunday of the month, Lorena rode Whiskey to the river once the sun was up enough to warm the air. The grassy bank was flooded where she undressed to swim. The beaver had built their dam higher, entwining willow branches in a complicated maze daubed with mud. One of the season's last robins soft-chirped from a cottonwood. Lorena swam circles in the small pool, then floated on her back, letting the blue abyss of the sky absorb into her eyes.

Jesse's shirt, still damp, clung to her skin when she put it on. She sat for a while ruffling her hair in an errant breeze to help it dry. In her mind she heard a fragment of the melody Jesse had sung to her, and standing, she took hold of his imaginary arms and danced in the grass with her eyes closed, her feet sinking into the wet earth.

Whiskey's nicker from where he was tied stopped her. The jingle of a bridle and the tiny creak of saddle leather made her open her eyes with the slow hope that her daydreaming had conjured Jesse back. Instead, she saw Clancy Melville sitting a tall black gelding.

"Morning," he said.

"Mr. Melville," she said.

"I think you need a partner, Lorena."

"No, thank you, I'm done dancing for the day," she said.

For a moment they stared at one another. A chill started at the base of Lorena's neck, snaked down her spine and iced her feet. She turned her back, took off Jesse's shirt and placed it carefully on a willow branch before moving toward the clothes she'd left near the river's edge.

She heard Clancy Melville step off his horse, and turned to see him leave his reins trailing so the black could graze. As he walked towards her she stepped into her pantaloons and reached for her chemise.

"I don't work on Sundays, Mr. Melville," she said.

"So Mabel told me," he said.

"I can see you next Saturday at your regular time."

"Certainly," he said. "But you'll also see me now. You work when I say you work."

"I don't work for you. I work for Mabel. I will not—"

He backhanded her to the ground. She turned her head away, tried to make her muscles move enough to crawl. She could not cry out, could not force herself to struggle or fight back, not even when his fist found her face again. Jesse. Where was Jesse? He said he'd come back.

"Whore," Melville spat, smashing her again. "Bitch. No one refuses me. Do you hear? No one."

His hands at her throat were cold, the thumbs pressing hard into her windpipe. Then black shapes flapped before her dimming eyes like a flock of migrating crows.

5.

The first thing Jesse saw when he rounded the river bend was something white fluttering from a willow. His mare spotted it and shied sideways, nearly unseating him.

"Daisy," he crooned, "easy girl, easy." He stroked her neck and stared as the mare backed away.

As the dusk light edged into total darkness, Jesse identified the object as a white shirt. A beaver swimming an A-line across the silver-mirrored surface of the pond smacked its flat tail in warning and dove. The mare jumped, then settled, snorting. A horse concealed in shadows whinnied a reply. Jesse took in the scene: a yellow and gold sprigged dress still draped by the water's edge and Lorena sprawled on the muddy ground, pantaloons torn, chemise still clutched in her hand. For a split second, Jesse thought she was sleeping, but the air was cold, the stars beginning to seep out as the last of the light disappeared, and he knew she was dead. The mare snorted again and backed up.

His intestines twisted, torment doubling him over the pommel. He closed his eyes and let his weight sink back against the cantle. His arms and legs tingled, then went numb. Behind his quivering eyelids, a vision of Lorena shimmered. She was dancing in his white shirt, her legs and feet bare, her head tilted up so that her hair hung loose along her back. He sat unmoving until the image faded, the pain receded, and he could breathe again. He thought of the miles he'd traveled during the months just past, how he'd fought the urge to return like a drunk fights the bottle. He thought of the scum who had done this and he wanted to feel bones break under his fists, wanted to see blood gush, wanted to hear someone beg for mercy. But what he wanted even more was peace, some sort of goodness and grace that would save him from himself. He'd come back for that. Now she was gone.

He rode a wide circle around the body, untied the dun, and turned it loose toward town. Then, easing the mare back, he plucked the shirt from its willow hanger. He held it, fresh-washed and crinkle-dried, to his face and inhaled. Fragrant soap, river water, sunshine, and Lorena's scent were all caught in the folds. Tucking the shirt inside his buckskin coat, he turned Daisy with slow deliberation and rode back the way he had come.

6.

"Uncle Jess?" Fenner asked adding another stick to the small fire he'd built up against a huge slab of sky-tilted granite.

"Yes, boy?"

"I thought we were goin' on to town to meet Mabel like you said. You promised we'd have chicken fried steak and a bed to sleep in."

"We will, Fen. Just not tonight. I got some things I got to think about."

"What kind of things?" Fenner asked.

"Man stuff," Jesse said, knowing that he couldn't very well say cold-blooded murder. "You go on and tend the horses. Tie Daisy good. This is her home country.

She might remember and want to go on back to the stable where I got her. Just hobble Harley. He'll be fine grazing around."

"Uncle Jess?" Fenner persisted.

"Hmmm, boy?"

"You seem awful sad."

"Guess I am," Jesse said as he pounded thin strips of jerked meat to add to a simmering pot that floated a few wild onions. "I guess I am."

"Is it because of my mama dying and all that?"

"Partly. I was mighty fond of your ma; she was a good sister to me."

"Are you sad 'cause you got stuck with me?"

Jesse stopped messing with the sack of coffee and stood up, dusting his hands on the seat of his worn pants. "Come here," he said, opening his right arm in a half circle.

Fenner scrambled into the embrace, his face smashing against Jesse's chest. He was big for a twelve year old, tall and rough-boned like a draft horse colt. Everything seemed too large a fit for the boy, his head, his ears, his hands, his feet. Even the tears that seeped out of his eyes, big drops of saltwater soaking Jesse's shirt, seemed too gigantic for one so young to bear.

"My ma," Fenner cried. "My ma. My ma."

Jesse patted his back with slip-shod tenderness. His sister dying of pneumonia had put everybody and everything in a tailspin. Fenner's father missing in the war; surely after all these years dead and gone and of no use to anyone, least of all to a boy who had only a toddler's misplaced memory. Jesse had tried to fill in for him, returning to the lowland farm whenever he drifted back east to visit, but he'd never been much good at sticking around. His restlessness drove him like a goad, the wonder of what might be around the next turn in the trail like fire under his feet. Moving on was his motto. If he kept chasing the wind, the ghosts of who and what he'd been would never catch up. Now though, through no fault of his own, he had two more specters searching for him in the night: Fenner's mother, his only sibling, and Lorena, the girl with the spun-gold hair lying crushed in the mud on the riverbank. His eyes filled to spilling and he pushed Fenner away as kindly as he could.

"Go on now, tend to Daisy and Harley, then we'll eat."

"But Uncle Jesse," Fenner choked.

"It's okay, Fen. I never had no boy of my own, so I might as well thank whatever gods there are that your mama left you to me. We're gonna be just fine. Just fine. Soon as we get some stew and coffee in our bellies, we're gonna be just fine."

———•———

The boy slept, his face soft in the rose-red glow of dying embers. Daisy dozed, halter-tied and hip-cocked just beyond the ring of firelight, a breathy huh-huh escaping her nostrils. Somewhere near the creek Harley ground grass between his teeth, his hobbles chinking with each tentative step. Jesse did not sleep. He stretched against his banged up McClellen saddle and fondled the white shirt his sister had made for him when he returned from the war. His fingers traced the small, tight stitches, the gathers at yoke and cuffs, the smooth glaze of polished antler buttons. He'd had so little love in his fast dash-and-run-for-the-woods kind of life, and this was what was left of it: a shirt he thought he'd stripped off and buried, a shirt Lorena had not only saved and laundered, but worn. He tried to imagine what it would have been like to sleep with her each night, to have her lithe, naturally perfumed body cradled in his arms, to wake to the wonder of her shining hair spread on a clean white pillow case trimmed with frilly lace. Nothing but well-washed cotton and a bunch of painful memories, he stretched the shirt toward the last flickers of fire. A twist of the wrist, one quick poof, and it would be gone, just as everything else he'd ever counted on had disappeared.

Jesse stared at Fenner bunched up in a fetal curl on a damp horse blanket, his boots and clothes still on, his slicker thrown over his shoulders for a ragtag bit of warmth against the autumn chill. The boy deserved better. He deserved the schooling his ma had started him with and maybe some church. He deserved a chance to have a wife, a passel of kids, a respected place in a community, a reputation that couldn't be ripped apart like a flag in a tornado wind. Folding the shirt in half, then rolling it loosely, Jesse placed it under his head, slid down, and swiveled his hips searching for a comfortable hollow. He welcomed an hour or two of sleep, though he didn't know why he expected or even hoped for that. He had not slept more than a catnap's worth for twenty years. It's what killing did to a man. Made it so he couldn't sleep, not even when he was so blasted tired his eyes felt like they held all the sand in west Texas. He tried to pray the prayer his mother had taught him down on his knees, his hands folded, his eyes closed, but the first words of the "Our Father" sounded stupid and sacrilegious. Jesse settled for "Keep us safe. Amen," and prepared himself for the onslaught of bloody dreams that never went away, the herd of nightmares he kept trying to outrace.

7.

"Christ Almighty, Jesse, you scared the living daylights out of me," Hobbes said, coming around the corner of the board and batten barn.

"Sorry, Hobbes, didn't think I should waltz down Main Street and in the front door," Jesse said.

"No way, you better keep yourself to the shadows, or better yet, get the hell on out of here. Melville's trying to . . .ah, Jesus, Jesse, do you even know what happened to Miss Lorena."

"I know," Jesse said, "that's why I've come back. That and I needed a home place for my boy here."

"That your boy back there? I didn't know you had a boy."

"Sister's boy. Mine now that she passed on."

"Jesse, you can't hang around here. Melville is trying to pin Miss Lorena's killing on you. He's been spewing lies like those geysers I heard about up in Yellowstone."

"That son-of-a-bitch. All the more reason for me—"

"Jesse, I'm telling you, get out. Flint's convinced you're the troublemaker. He's laying for you."

"Okay, Hobbes, listen. Just keep Daisy and Harley inside for me."

"Hey, is that my gray mare?" Hobbes asked smiling.

"Sorry, Hobbes, I was kinda in a rush last time I was here."

"No problem. I always figured you'd bring her back someday."

"Fenner," Jesse said, waving the boy forward on the blue roan gelding. "This here's Mr. Hobbes. He's going to keep the horses for us. Bring your slicker and saddlebags. We're going to get us some chicken fried steak."

"Jesse, I'm warning you," Hobbes said as he took the twin set of reins and led the pair of ponies into the dark recesses of the stable.

"Everything's fine, Hobbes. Everything's going to be just fine now. You got your mare back. Fenner's gonna get his chicken fried steak. Mabel's gonna be real glad to see me. And, Melville, well Melville's going to find out what it means to get the short end of a stick for a change."

"What's that mean, Uncle Jess?" Fenner asked.

"Never mind, boy. It doesn't matter."

8.

The girls clustered in the dusty courtyard behind Mabel's like a bunch of chickens scratching after feed. Squawking chatter interspersed with giggles filled the sun-speckled air beneath a few leafless cottonwood trees. Sagging clothes-lines tied from branch to branch waved wrappers and slips, chemises and panta-loons, stockings and flounced skirts. A calico cat lay in a puddle of shade while her trio of month-old kittens danced after leaves skittering in front of a gust-and-sigh breeze.

"Cover up, gals," Jesse said walking through the gate, rifle in hand, buckskin coat over his shoulder. "I'm bringing along a boy."

"Jesse," they piped in harmony. "Who's this? Where'd you find such a handsome lad? Look at those sea-green eyes."

"This here's Fenner. Where's Mabel?"

"Right here, you lazy, good-for-nothing, low-down, sneaking up behind my back rascal," Mabel said sliding her bulk sideways out the door. Jesse scooped her up and held her off the ground like she was a teenager. He twirled her around and around as she squealed childish delight making the other women laugh. Fenner stepped back and squatted down to tickle the cat's ears, making her purr.

"We're here for some chicken fried steak. And a bath. And a bed if you got one to spare," Jesse said.

"We do. We do," Mabel said, her face blushed and radiant. "But Jesse—"

"Don't you go, 'but Jesseing' me. I know all there is to know, or near about. The rest will wait."

"Okay, then. Sophie, you go sit on the front stoop and keep an eye out. Val, you stay out here in back and watch. We've got a couple hours until opening. Let's get these boys something to eat."

Mabel winked at Fenner and ushered him through the door. "Your sister's boy?" she asked Jesse. He nodded.

"Gone?" she asked.

"Pneumonia. About a month ago."

"No other kin?"

"None. Just me…and now you."

"Ah, Jesse," Mabel began.

"Come on, Mabel. He's still a boy. He's gonna need some mothering, some guidance. I can't do this all on my own."

"But here?"

"Why not? He'll have these gals to sister him, lots of tender loving care, music, laughter, chores to do. Surely you can find some work to help him pay his way."

"Jesse, you exasperate the hell out of me. Every time I turn around you're interfering with my life, not to mention my heart."

"It's what I'm good at Mabel. Stirring up trouble," he said and kissed the top of her henna-red curls.

9.

They pushed back their plates, each of them groaning from the weight of steak, potatoes and gravy, dried apple pie and black, black coffee. Jesse swirled a ring of whiskey around a glass and watched while Mabel interrogated Fenner with the usual new-kid-on-the-block questions. Fenner looked over at Jesse with a forlorn please-rescue-me expression tugging at the corners of his mouth and exhausted eyes.

"Need a bath and a bed?" Jesse asked him.

"Yes, please, Uncle Jess. I'm mighty tired."

Mabel called Sophie in from the front porch and asked her to fill the tub. Steaming pots of water already waited on the wood stove. "Give that boy what he needs, then leave him be. He's too young for you to be messing around with him. Show him the way upstairs to Lorena's old room. It's got the best bed."

"Sophie back?" Jesse asked.

"Yeah. For now. Baxter's gone on north with a herd for the Box R."

"She working?"

"No, just helping out. Got too lonely for her out there at the line shack alone."

"Melville after her again?"

"Not really, Jesse. He's polite enough. Spends most of his time with Val or Sassy."

"He do it?"

"Jesse, you can't ask me— "

"I can. And I am. Did he kill her?"

Mabel looked him square in the face, faded indigo eyes boring into deep hazel, but she didn't blink or utter another word.

"Good enough, Mabel. I know all I need to know. Christ! One day earlier and everything would be different. One day? Damn. One hour. One blessed god-for-saken pitiful hour."

He tossed back the last sip of whiskey and dropped his head on his folded hands. A shudder surged through his body and he sighed, an exhalation of breath so gigantic the table rocked. Mabel stood and placed her palm between his shoulder blades.

"She loved you, Jesse. For some silly, unknown, ridiculous reason, she loved you. And she was waiting for you to come back. She was counting on you to come back."

"I know that, Mabel. I heard her calling me. Night after night. Day after day. All those miles and I heard her calling me back. Jesse. Jesse. She said my name like a god-damned prayer."

"Can't you just forget it now. Leave it be. Take your boy and go somewhere new, where no one knows you, where you won't have to be looking behind your back every minute."

"I can't, Mabel. I won't. I'm sick to death of being haunted by the people I've failed."

The back door scraped open. Flint pushed Val inside the room ahead of him. Mabel opened her arms and Val rushed to her saying "Miss Mabel, I tried to—"

"It's okay, Sugar," Mabel said. "Flint," she nodded.

Flint nodded back, tipping his hat. Jesse had not moved other than to sit upright in the straight-back chair.

"Carlson," the sheriff said, nodding at Jesse.

"Sheriff," Jesse said, keeping both his hands on the knife-scarred tabletop.

"Staying long?"

"Just long enough to get my boy settled in here with Mabel. I'd like to have enough time to file on a section of ground for him, see about some schooling."

"Your boy?" Flint asked.

"My sister's. Mine now that she's gone."

"I ought to lock you up this minute and telegraph the federal judge," Flint said.

"Do what you have to do, Sheriff, but I'd like to have a little time. If you give me a bit of time, I'll come in myself. Get this over with once and for all."

"There isn't a reason in this world why I should trust you. Not after what happened around here."

"Don't blame Melville's dirt on me, Flint. I may not be the most Christian man riding these hills, but you know I'm not a murderer."

"Okay, Jesse," Flint said. "Three days. That's all. Melville's gone to Denver on some business. I want you in my office by sundown on Saturday."

"Good enough. I'll be there."

"You better be, or that boy's gonna lose his uncle as well as his ma."

10.

Crouched in a shadowed crevice between two boulders, Jesse searched his mind for anything he might have left undone. He'd been to the land office twice and found a parcel of quarter sections that held patches of pine timber, some high, dry sagebrush pasture, and a long sickle-shaped meadow with a narrow ribbon of willow-edged river winding through the native redtop. He found a surveyor and together with Fenner they went by wagon, a rag tied to one of the front spokes, and counted out the wheel revolutions to measure the boundaries. Then, they marked the corners with tepee-shaped piles of stone. From the jagged edge of a small undercut cliff, Jesse studied the lay of the land, spotting the beaver pond where he had bathed, the bank where he and Lorena had danced, the place where he'd found her body. He asked the surveyor if the big beaver house was on the place and was assured that it was. "This," Jesse told Fenner, "will be a good spot for a house someday."

Just as the sun came up the following morning he'd visited the cemetery on the rock-studded hill behind the white-painted building they called the church and found the week-old grave decorated with a quart-size canning jar holding a bouquet of wilted sticky asters. There was nothing else to mark the place where Lorena lay under the earth, nothing but turned dirt and the sparkle of a few quartz-gilded stones catching the first light.

"You deserved better," Jesse said to the misty, cool air. "You deserved a husband and a home and a bunch of tow-headed toddlers."

There was more he wanted to say, but he couldn't find the right words and didn't know how he would have gotten them past the logjam in his throat if he had found them. He wanted to cry, but crying had never helped anything. It certainly hadn't saved his folks or their burned out farm. It for sure hadn't mattered to the men and horses cut down all around him on the battlefields. So, instead, he stood there with his hat in his hand and let the sun warm his gray hair, let the whisper of wind coming up from the river bring back the feel of Lorena waltzing in his arms. That was prayer enough.

The girls at Mabel's had taken Fenner under their collective wings and in two days' time he was laughing and talking and carrying on like a boy wanting to be a man, proud of all the attention he was getting. Jesse wasn't worried about Fenner; he knew Mabel would see to him like her own son, like the child she'd lost twenty some years ago, her first and only, the one she wept over for weeks, the one she claimed was Jesse's, but he'd never been certain of the fact even though Mabel swore he was her only beau. Women. Women. The way they complicated the world amazed him. If it weren't for women he wouldn't be trying to take care of things for Fenner and he wouldn't be squashed here between two standing stones waiting for nightfall. He watched the deepening twilight. Now that the sun had slipped behind the hogback to the west, he had a good wide view of the two-rut road and nothing to obscure or interrupt the angle of his intention. He'd only have one chance to do this thing right, and if it were the last thing he ever did, he'd do it the way it should have been done a long time back.

His money was deposited at the bank, along with a fast-scratched will leaving all his worldly goods to his sister's son. He laughed at that. His money in a bank. Not that there was much, but it seemed a funny ending for a Yankee payroll and the proceeds from the sale of a string of one hundred and sixty Union branded horses down in Mexico. He could still see his partners swinging from a cottonwood tree, a blood-red slash of sun swaying in and out of view between the bodies. He could still hear Melville's high-pitched voice screaming, "You're next, Carlson. You're next."

Jesse shrugged his shoulders and tugged at the wide, white cuffs of his shirt. He wished he'd brought his buckskin coat to ward off the chill settling in his hands. Another ten minutes and his light would be gone, his guess that Melville would be coming on into town tonight wrong. He'd listened close to the gossip, paid attention to what folks said about Melville's habits, heard Mabel tell Sophie to make sure the bar was picked up and polished because the boss was expected to return. He'd spent plenty of time earlier in the afternoon scouting out his spot, looking for just the right location to afford him the advantage of close range and surprise. He'd even asked Hobbes if Melville was still riding the rangy black. He'd done all he could do to get his cards laid out straight. Now the rest was up to sweet Miss Destiny.

He turned at the sound of a nighthawk's single shriek, and when he glanced back Clancey Melville's black paced up the road, kicking tiny red plumes of dust around its ankles. Jesse waited. He waited until he could see Melville's face under his hat, until he could see his right hand loose on the split reins. Then he leapt, three bounding steps down into the road, and skidded to a stop, pistol drawn.

"Get down," he said at the same time the black half reared and snorted.

Clancey Melville obeyed the order, slipping his right foot from the stirrup and swinging that leg over the cantle toward the ground as his gelding's front feet came to rest again. Jesse didn't hesitate a hair's breadth. The second Melville's hand left the saddle horn Jesse shot him through the palm saying "that's for hanging innocent men." The next shot caught Melville in the groin, blew him backwards with his left foot still in the stirrup. "That's for Lorena who didn't deserve a coward like you touching her," Jesse said as he grabbed the black's reins to keep him from bolting and dragging Melville. "And this," Jesse said, as he kicked Melville's foot free of the stirrup and turned loose the horse, "is to send you to hell without having to suffer." The last shot took out Melville's temple. "After all," Jesse said kicking dirt at the still body, "I am known to be a kind man."

He heard horses behind him, but did not turn. The black raced toward them, head held to the side to avoid stepping on the dragging reins. Jesse stood, pistol at his left side and stared at the man he'd wanted to kill ever since he could remember. Dead now, but it didn't make anything right. Killing never did. Even so, something tight-coiled in his gut unwound, slithered down his legs into the blackness at his feet and crawled off into the encroaching night. He felt it gone and knew he was free again.

"Jesse," he heard Flint say from a safe distance, "Throw it down and turn around."

"He ain't just gonna give up, Sheriff," he heard another voice whisper.

Jesse considered his options. He only had two. Prison was one. A stand of dog-hair jack pine stood silhouetted against the very last light. Twenty, maybe thirty feet away. Darkness. A bit of luck. Another hug from sweet Miss Destiny. He stared at the spot, thought he saw a shimmer of white moving just beyond the nearest whip-thin trunks. His left shoulder flinched.

"Don't do it, Carlson," Flint warned. "You've run out of chances. Turn around."

Jesse turned and as he turned he raised his pistol in a single fluid motion and fired toward the blue-black velvet of the sky. Other pistols shouted stop. Several shots whizzed past him high on the left. Another caught him on the side of the neck severing the artery. Stunned, he still spun to run, but his knees buckled and he crumpled face down in the dirt.

———•———

"Check him, Hobbes," Flint said. "Get his gun."

Hobbes holstered his unfired pistol. He climbed off his horse, handed the reins to Flint, then walked over to Jesse, kneeled down and took the weapon from his hand.

"Shit, Jesse," Hobbes said, "That was a stupid thing to do."

"Hobbes," Jesse murmured.

"It's me, all right."

"Give my shirt to the boy. His ma made it."

"Sure thing, Jesse," Hobbes said and took hold of his hand.

Hobbes wished he could think of a prayer for Jesse but the only words that came to him were from a song he used to sing before he lost his arm:

> It matters little now, Lorena
> The past is in the eternal past
> Our hearts will soon lie low, Lorena
> Life's tide is ebbing out so fast
> There is a future, oh, thank God!
> Of life this is so small a part
> 'Tis dust to dust beneath the sod
> But there, up there, 'tis heart to heart.

Hobbes felt Jesse give a little squeeze, then a cold, still silence settled all around them.

11.

When Mabel opened the back door and saw Hobbes standing there with the blood stained shirt, she did nothing except close her eyes, her fists clenched at her sides. Hobbes called out "Sophie" and the girl came and took Mabel and led her to a chair and sat her down.

"Where's the boy?" Hobbes asked.

"Upstairs in his room," Sophie said.

Hobbes climbed the spur-scarred stairs with care, his stump useless above the banister. When he reached the door of Lorena's old room, he knocked twice, firm and polite. Fenner opened the door and bronze lamplight flooded the hallway. Hobbes held out the shirt to him and said, "He wanted you to have it." A copy of *Longfellow's Complete Poems* fell from Fenner's hand to the floor.

"Take it, boy. At least it's something to remember him by."

Fenner reached out and took the wadded cotton. Hobbes clutched Fenner's bony young shoulder for a moment, then turned and made his slow way back down the stairs.

———

Fenner picked up the book he had dropped and placed it on the dresser. He gathered the shirt to his chest with both hands and held it, the hard copper smell of drying blood needling his nostrils.

Lying back on the bed, he allowed the tears to come, let them trace their way toward his ears which rang with buzzing emptiness, soundless tears, tears with no crying or sobbing, no choking or sniffling. Not a boy's tears, a man's tears.

The calico cat stirred behind the window's lace curtain, jumped from the sill to the foot of the bed and tiptoed up Fenner's leg and onto his belly. She lay there, eyes half closed, until he reached up and scratched her behind the ears. She began to purr, her paws flexing and contracting, massaging his ribs, soothing his caged, fast-beating heart.

Contributors

Teague Bohlen teaches creative writing at the University of Colorado–Denver, where he serves as contributing editor to *Copper Nickel*. His short fiction has most recently been seen in *Terrain.org* and *The Yellow Rake*, and he is a regular contributor to *Bias*, among other regional and national magazines. His first novel, *The Pull of the Earth*, from which the chapter in this collection is taken, is coming out in 2006 from Ghost Road Press. He is currently at work on both a book of short stories, called *Map of Town*, and a new novel, tentatively titled *Pizza Guy*.

When she is not writing, poet **Laurie Wagner Buyer** hikes in the high country, teaches with Writers on the Net, or devotes time to her mentoring and editing business Creative Adventure: A Guide Service for Writers. Her new collection of poetry, *Across the High Divide*, has just been released from Ghost Road Press.

> The idea for "Miss Lorena's Nightshirt" came about because I had a lifelong phobia about going into bars and saloons. Even when I was with friends, I would never enter a drinking establishment first. One night, following my mother into her local tavern, I experienced an unnerving vision of a woman's death on a riverbank. When I gathered my composure and returned home, I sat quietly and asked the woman who she was and why she'd come to me. She told me her story in bits and pieces. All I had to do was ask, listen, and write down what I saw and heard. "Miss Lorena's Nightshirt" turned into the first chapter of my new novel titled *Woman in White*.

Linda Frantzen Carlson wrote a personal observation column for almost eight years (January 1992–August 1999) for the *Boulder Daily Camera* in Boulder; and between 1982 and 1992, she published more than thirty pieces, including play reviews, feature articles, satire, and poetry, for various local publications, in addition to selling several greeting card ideas to Hallmark. In October 1999, her first book—a humorous look at life in the "fat lane," titled *Plump: Survival of the Fattest*—was published by White-Boucke Publishing. Her poetry has been published in *Möbius*, *Pegasus*, and *Art Times* and recently some of her poetry has been chosen for publication in *Poetry Motel*. She loves words in any format, loves her family and friends, loves Colorado, but camping, not so much.

Mary Domenico lives in Denver with her husband Howard and her talented children, Kate and Daniel.

Where does any story come from? I'm a periodic insomniac. I was afraid of the dark as a child. I used to be a psychotherapist and for several years I ran a shelter for homeless girls. As a young woman, I lived in an old Victorian in downtown Denver and took cabs home when it was too cold to walk. I wrote *The Dark* partly in rebellion against conventions that dictate certain forms for narratives, especially story arcs that lead to resolutions and illustrations of meaning. My own life has been a chaotic juxtaposition of mostly unresolved events, some of which repeat certain themes, none of which has ever, in fifty years, revealed the slightest substantive statement concerning life's meaning. I think fiction that matters stays in the realm of ambiguity, refuses the consolation of glib interpretation, and at best offers some slight opportunity for new insight by mirroring the human conditions of complexity and uncertainty.

Alison Flowers was born in England to an American military family, relocating frequently during her childhood until the age of ten when her family settled in Denver. Flowers was home-educated for five years by her mother, who encouraged her to write creatively. She received her undergraduate degree in French from Regis University and obtained a similar degree from the University of Paris IV–Sorbonne, where she lived, studied, and wrote for a year in 2003. "A Bird, Yabba" reflects her travel and international experiences, her friendships with Arabs and Muslims, and the prejudice against them in American society.

Matt Hudson graduated from Vermont College's MFA in Writing program. He moved to Colorado about two years ago and began thinking about creating this collection shortly thereafter. He currently works as an editor in Boulder, and his fiction has recently appeared in *Matter*. He is also a contributing editor of *Hunger Mountain*.

Mark Hummel was born and raised in Wyoming and has lived in northern Colorado with his wife and three daughters for seventeen years. His fiction and essays have appeared or are forthcoming in *The Bloomsbury Review*, *Fugue*, *Matter*, *Porcupine Literary Arts Magazine*, *Talking River*, *Tar Wolf Review*, and elsewhere. He teaches creative writing at the University of Northern Colorado. He is completing work on *Water Cycle*, an alternatively structured novel in the form of linked stories that share common characters and a fictional Colorado setting. "Confluence" is from the *Water Cycle* series.

Nate Liederbach lives in Gunnison, Colorado. In March 2005, Ghost Road Press released his short story collection *Doing a Bit of Bleeding*.

Chris Ransick's first book, *Never Summer*, won a Colorado Book Award for poetry in 2003. His subsequent collection of short stories, *A Return to Emptiness*, won the 2005 Colorado Authors' League Fiction Award and was a finalist for the 2005 Colorado Book Award in fiction. His forthcoming collection of poetry, *Lost Songs & Last Chances*, will be published by Ghost Road Press in August 2006. Chris lives in Englewood with his wife, son, and daughter.

A. Rooney has been writing professionally for over thirty years as a columnist, feature writer, magazine editor, and publisher, as well as corporate writer. His fiction and nonfiction have been published widely. He teaches writing at the University of Denver and the University of Colorado–Denver. His first collection of stories is titled *The Colorado Motet*.

Carol Samson teaches literature and creative writing courses at the University of Denver. She is at work on a book-length volume of short stories titled *Among Twenty Snowy Mountains*.

Acknowledgments

I would like to thank all of the folks at Black Ocean for their extensive support, particularly Janaka Stucky and Carrie Adams. Heather Sutphin is responsible for the design and layout of this collection, and Dennis Collier has provided significant publishing guidance along the way. Thank you.

I would also like to thank Brian, Marie, Harrison, and Mary for their outstanding critiques; Lee Idleman for his support; and, of course, my parents and A.

What's your impossible?